JOSIAH

WILLIAM MALMBORG

DARKER DREAMS MEDIA

ISBN - 978-1-7348763-2-1

JOSIAH

PART ONE

THE GIRL IN THE STRAITJACKET

ONE

JOSIAH COULD FEEL the grime of the soiled carpet between his toes as he stepped from the steamy bathroom toward the bed where his clothes were waiting, disgust with Joel and the filth that he had wallowed in on a daily basis dominating his mind.

How could his friend live like this?

How could he stand to walk around, or sit, or sleep in it?

His skin crawled just thinking about it.

And then there was the kitchen.

Josiah had seen some fucked-up shit in his lifetime, but nothing had been as bad as that. It was as if Joel had no concept of using a garbage can and simply set stuff on the counters until there was no space left. Rinsing things off also seemed a foreign concept to him, the plates and bowls that were stacked in the sink and next to it looking as if the leftover food smudges and chunks had been allowed to harden for days, if not weeks.

It was disgusting.

Joel was disgusting.

And making it all worse, Josiah had been forced to search

through the mess to find a carving knife, one that he eventually found in an old greasy pizza box that had been set atop a pan on the stove, flies erupting from within when he lifted the lid, thanks to the four pieces that had been left to rot.

It had made him want to vomit.

Still did.

Things like the kitchen experience imprinted themselves upon his mind. He would be thinking about it for days, weeks, maybe even months. It was like seeing wild dogs eating bodies in the backstreets of Baghdad. They always went for the genitals first, the rectum second, digging their teeth in and ripping out whatever they could pull free. Such sights did not go away. At least not for him. And talking about them did not help. He had tried, the military having insisted he see a head doctor after the *incident*, but nothing positive had resulted.

The Father on the other hand...

Josiah shook his head.

The Father wouldn't want to hear about this. All he cared about was the mission and whether Josiah successfully completed it.

The answer to that was yes.

At least it would be as soon as he took out the trash and got into the car and drove away.

Once that was done—

Downstairs he heard a door open.

Josiah froze.

"Dad?" a female voice called.

What?

No!

Joel wasn't supposed to be having any company that night, especially not the whore of a daughter who lived with her whore of a mother.

That was why that night had been perfect.

Joel would be alone, and the next day was trash day.

No!

No!

No!

"Dad?" she called again from the front room.

Josiah turned and looked toward the trash bags that were in the bathroom doorway, and then at the clothes he had left on the bed so they wouldn't get dirty while he was dismembering Joel in the bathtub.

Maybe she'll leave.

If not...

He didn't know what to do.

"DAD?" Mel called for a third time.

Nothing.

She waited several seconds.

"Dad?"

Again, nothing.

She sighed and headed toward the kitchen, her throat still raw from the shouting match she and her mom had engaged in earlier that evening, one that had ended with her grabbing her backpack and walking out.

Her mother didn't try to stop her.

She never did.

She and her boy toy Todd liked it when she was gone.

And Mel preferred being gone.

Everybody wins.

Of course, knowing they liked it when she was gone, Todd especially, she sometimes would stay just to piss them off. Tonight was not one of those nights. It couldn't be. Not after what she had discovered in the trash when dropping in a bag from McDonald's. Nope. It was one thing to accept that her mother and her boy toy Todd were fucking, but to realize he had managed to knock her up. That was too much. Making it worse, her mother said she was keeping it.

Keeping it.

A forty-five-year-old woman.

Keeping the baby of a twenty-two-year-old boy toy.

Mel couldn't even begin to comprehend it.

It was too fucked up.

Shaking her head, Mel opened the door into the kitchen and stepped inside, the smell of rot hitting her full force.

"Jesus butt fuck!" she snapped and stepped back out, hand pressed to her nose.

Three weeks ago, she had helped her dad by cleaning the kitchen, his continuing depression over the failed marriage having once again gotten the better of him. This, however, was ten times worse than it had been that weekend, and was at the point where she didn't think she could do it. He needed help. Professional help. They both did. Her father was a slob who couldn't seem to get it together after the divorce, and her mother was on her way to becoming a nymphomaniac who couldn't get enough of her twenty-two-year-old boy toy. Could things get any crazier?

Probably, an inner voice warned.

She looked at the kitchen door and prepared to go back in, her throat needing something to soothe it after all the shouting. Coke, root beer, Snapple, whiskey...anything, just as long as it was cool and wet.

Deep breath.

And a second.

And a third.

She pushed open the door, body beelining for the fridge.

Like the kitchen itself, the inside was a cesspool of rotting leftovers and packages of meat that had been bought but never opened, the use-by dates likely having come and gone.

Several cans of Coke were present as well.

She grabbed one and hurried out of the kitchen, her lungs feeling as if they were going to burst.

Deep breath.

She popped the top and chugged half of the sweet beverage.

A belch followed, as did a sigh of satisfaction.

JOSIAH STOOD FROZEN in the master bedroom, his ears listening as the daughter moved around the house, her body eventually settling in the room just two doors down from the one he was currently standing in, naked, his clothes still laid out on the bed.

He didn't know what to do.

His instructions had only concerned Joel.

He was the only one who was supposed to be in the house, the only one who was supposed to die.

But now...

Plans change.

It was a lesson he had learned over and over again while in the military.

When one went out beyond the wire, he needed to be ready to adapt to whatever events unfolded.

This was no different.

He was out beyond the wire.

He was—

Joel's phone rang, a familiar soundtrack from some movie that Josiah could not immediately place echoing within the room.

Shit!

MEL HEARD the musical ringtone playing in her dad's room as she held her own phone to her ear, and looked toward the open bedroom door, confusion turning to dismay and then concern.

If his phone was here...

"Dad?" she called, voice loud enough to carry throughout the house.

Nothing.

She ended the call, the musical ringtone dying, and walked to the doorway of her room.

"Dad?" she called again, even though she knew she wouldn't get a response. "You okay?"

Again, nothing.

The house was silent.

Something wasn't right.

An uneasy feeling began to develop.

She stepped into the hallway, her voice nearly calling out again, but then decided against it given how fruitless such actions had already been. Instead, she simply stood where she was, staring at the open door of her dad's bedroom, listening.

Thoughts on his depression appeared.

The marriage had ended nearly two years earlier, yet he still wasn't over it, especially now that her mom was fucking that boy toy. And given the state of the kitchen, these last couple of weeks had been a struggle, so...

No.

As depressed as he had been, he wouldn't hurt himself.

Never.

He might wallow in filth and put on weight while binging Netflix during his non-working hours, but that was as far as he would go. Stuffing his face with pizza day in and day out was all the harm he would do to himself. Going beyond that...

Loved ones always say this...

Fear appeared.

Call the police.

No.

Not yet.

If he had simply gone out to get something without taking his phone and the police showed up, her bitch of a mom would use the state of the kitchen to hurt the joint custody agreement they currently had. She would claim it was to protect Mel, but really it would just be so she could renegotiate the terms of alimony, which, despite the fact that she had ended the marriage herself because she had been fucking other people, had favored her.

All because of me.

Mel had gotten to choose who she would live with, and not wanting to change schools, had picked her mom, who was getting to keep the house.

She shook her head.

What was done was done.

She could not take back the decisions she had made.

No one could.

But she could try to make sure she didn't fuck up her father's life again by bringing the police into a situation that they were not needed in.

NAKED, Josiah stood by the bedroom door, waiting, listening, his mind trying to figure out what the daughter's next move would be, his hands ready to grab her the moment she stepped through the doorway.

And then what?

A vision of himself throwing her onto the bed so that he could get atop her unfolded within his mind, his manhood firming up as he anticipated the feel of her throat in his hands while he straddled her.

The Father would not approve.

It would be one thing to kill her, but to do so in a way that brought about sexual gratification...

Such actions were not tolerated.

Ever.

He would be punished.

Severely.

With flame.

And it wouldn't be his forearms that would suffer.

No.

He shivered, his manhood shrinking a bit at the thought but not going away completely.

And then the question on what to do with her returned, a sound that might have been her stepping toward the room reaching his ears.

MEL STARTED toward her dad's bedroom, concern about what she might find within growing with each step.

Please be empty.

Please be empty.

Please be empty.

She stepped through the open doorway, phone in hand, ready to call 911, anger toward her mom and her recent actions in tormenting him with her Facebook posts about how much she loved boy toy Todd ready to be unleashed.

The light in the master bath was on and illuminated part of the room.

Three black garbage bags sat in the center of the floor.

What the...?

She spun to the right, arms rising to ward off the movement she sensed, a huge hand managing to grab her throat before she could scream.

He was like something from a nightmare, a giant in human form that lifted her from her feet while slamming her back into the wall, her fingernails doing little to penetrate the scarred flesh that encircled his arms, all while her lungs struggled to suck in air through the throat he was squeezing.

And then she was thrown to the floor, her body actually bouncing as it hit the carpet, a heavy numbness spreading throughout her limbs.

She blinked and tried to breathe, but her lungs seemed frozen from the impact, a horrific wheeze all she could manage.

He loomed over her, the light from the bathroom failing to reveal his features, yet doing enough for her to see that he truly was a giant. A naked giant, his penis straining.

No! No! No!

He got down on the floor with her, knees straddling her, hands going to her throat.

She tried to kick him while he did this, her target the testicles that dangled, but her legs would not move.

He squeezed.

Panic set in, her hands once again clawing at him as the life returned to them.

Her legs were also coming back, one of them finally able to deliver a blow to that tender area between his legs.

A grunt echoed.

She kicked again, but it had little effect as he lowered himself down to pin her to the floor.

"No!"

She didn't realize the cry was her own until his hands loosened from her throat.

She was able to breathe again.

She was—

A hand grabbed her by the hair, lifting her head several inches from the floor and then slamming it back down.

Bright yellow flashes appeared in the darkness.

A blink brought the room back.

He slammed her head again, bringing more sparks and a new heaviness to her body.

A third and fourth blow followed, her head feeling scrambled to the point where her brain might start oozing from her ears and nose.

A fifth blow brought unconsciousness.

JOSIAH STOOD STARING for several seconds before he managed to get control of himself and checked the girl for a pulse. She was alive, the thump of her heart easily felt when touching her chest.

You almost lost control, an inner voice said.

Actually, there was no almost about it. He had lost control, but then regained it before it went too far.

He shook his head, frustration with himself erupting.

Now what?

The garbage can only had room for one body, so cutting her up like Joel was not really an option.

Plus, he didn't want to kill her.

Instead, he wanted to—

Stop! he screamed at himself, his penis once again pointing straight ahead, fluid leaking from the tip.

Lighter, another voice said.

No.

Yes.

No.

Do it!

Now!

Without further delay, he went to his clothes and pulled the lighter from his pants pocket, his thumb flicking the striker.

A flame appeared, the light dancing on the walls.

He stared at it for a second and then looked down at the unconscious girl, the desires still present.

Taking a deep breath, he touched the flame to the underside of his left forearm, pain instantly erupting.

One Mississippi.

Two Mississippi.

Three Mississippi.

By *Thirty Mississippi*, tears were running down his cheeks, yet even so he kept the flame against the blackening flesh, the knuckles of that hand white as he kept his fingers fisted, his palms likely bleeding where his nails dug in.

At *Sixty Mississippi* he pulled the flame away, his finger letting it disappear while his body dropped to his knees, the tears unstoppable as he struggled to accept the pain, his mind begging the scorched nerve ending to stop firing so that he could complete his mission.

Such was not to be.

His desire had brought this on and now he had to endure while finishing up.

It was like being wounded.

Nothing would change it.

He had to keep going.

The girl moaned, her body twitching a bit.

Seeing this, Josiah stood back up and got the duct tape he had used while bagging Joel, the dismembered limbs having gone into one bag that was then completely enclosed with tape before going into a second bag, thus ensuring that even if something tore the outer bag, the inner taped-up bag would stay secure and wouldn't bring about suspicion.

The process had nearly used the entire roll, but there was still enough to secure the girl, her wrists being bound behind her back, then her ankles, and then her mouth, a decision on taking her with him so that the Father could advise on what he should do with her being made.

After that, he put his clothes back on, his shirt irritating the new burn, and then went about taking out the trash. Once that was done, he walked down the street to get his car so that he could back into the driveway and put the girl into the trunk.

MEL SMELLED something burning as she was lifted, her mind struggling to figure out what was going on. Nothing fully registered until she felt herself being set down. At that point the big man with the scars came into focus. She tried to scream but couldn't, her lips sealed. Her wrists were also secured, as were her ankles.

Darkness returned as something slammed.

It wasn't until she felt the bump of the curb that she realized she was in a trunk.

Oh God!

No! No! No!

She was being kidnapped!

It seemed completely unthinkable, yet that was exactly what had just happened.

He was kidnapping her.

TWO

JOSIAH DIDN'T GET a thrill from choking the chicken. It was too lifeless, too passive, almost as if it knew its purpose and accepted its fate.

People were never like that.

Even a wounded soldier on the battlefield who had been riddled with bullets and could feel his life oozing away with each passing second would struggle a bit once death came calling. But the chicken, which was in the prime of its life, didn't. It simply died.

Gramma Matilda was waiting for him in the yard behind the kitchen.

"Just one," she scoffed as he set the bird down on the old picnic table and began plucking feathers.

"One's enough."

"No, no, Betsy is coming with her boys. We need at least two, maybe three."

Josiah shook his head, his mind unsure who Betsy and the boys had been, and simply said, "That's tomorrow. Tonight it's just us."

"Oh," Gramma Matilda said, a look of confusion distorting her wrinkled face.

Josiah continued to pluck, his fingers working without thought while his mind once again began to wonder about the girl and what the decision would be. For nearly a week he had been waiting, his heart racing with anticipation each time he got a chance to speak with the Father, but every time he met with the man, nothing about the girl would be conveyed to him. It was frustrating because he felt that the Lord had put her in his path for a reason, one that needed to be revealed sooner rather than later given the risk that keeping her presented.

The Lord works in mysterious ways...

Josiah sighed.

Gramma Matilda mumbled something.

Josiah looked up and asked, "What?"

"Betsy's boys like corn. We should pick some extra corn."

Josiah let out a second sigh.

"And we'll need to make some biscuits."

"They're bringing the biscuits," Josiah said.

"Oh."

"And some apple pie."

"Betsy knows I don't like apple pie. She does this just to..." Her voice faded.

"Why don't you go back inside," Josiah said after a few seconds. "Rest up before Betsy and the boys get here."

Gramma Matilda didn't go inside. It wasn't an act of defiance or rejection of his suggestion. Instead, her face had taken on that glazed look that meant her mind had once again entered the fog.

Relief arrived.

Talking in circles with her was exhausting. He preferred the fogs.

And to be alone.

Wiping his hands on his pants, he stood up to help her back inside, a realization that she had pissed herself arriving as he took her arm to guide her.

He shook his head.

It never ended.

Either she was talking in circles as her mind brought up moments that had long since played out or she was wandering in the fog, pissing and shitting herself.

She needed to be in a nursing home where she could get professional care, but Britney would not allow it.

Nope.

Nursing homes cost money, even crappy ones that would let the old prune marinate in her own feces for hours, and money was not something Britney wanted to part with—not when it would cut into the eventual inheritance that all this land would provide once Gramma Matilda finally passed on.

ONE COULD NOT RUN out of tears. This was something Mel had learned during her time spent in the dusty second-floor room that overlooked what appeared to be an old farm field that had been left to rot. They just kept coming. And she didn't even know why. Despair? Fear? She had no idea. She also didn't know what he planned on doing with her but knew it had to be something elaborately horrific, for why else would he keep her locked in the old bedroom, body pretzeled into a straitjacket, mouth muzzled by a head harness, a ring in the upper back connected to a chain that was padlocked to the bed?

Simply keeping her like this day after day, feeding her and cleaning her, could not have been his motivation for taking her from her father's house. There had to be more. But what?

And who else was in the house?

Was it more girls like her? Ones he had abducted for some

unknown scheme, some game he would eventually play with them out in the field? Some sacrifice?

Or did he have a partner that never showed himself?

It didn't make any sense.

If he had raped her, she would have understood him and his motivations. Not that she wanted that. Not at all. But it would be something she understood. A motivation that was a part of the world she resided in. But this...this was different. This was something she could not comprehend. And because of that, she couldn't even begin to figure out what might come next.

And she could not escape.

She had tried, her body wiggling and twisting within the heavy canvas garment for hours, all to no avail. On TV it looked simple, the act of freeing oneself from such a jacket so *meh* that it was always the initial step in a much larger, more elaborate escape setup. But for her, it was the entire setup, one that she could not overcome. It was pathetic. She was pathetic. And scared.

Making things worse, her crotch burned.

It was the strap that did it.

All her struggles had rubbed things raw, and given how infrequently he cleaned her—especially down there—it was likely that whatever damage had occurred in her struggles had now gotten infected.

I should tell him.

Next time he was in there to feed her.

But then what?

He wasn't going to take her to a doctor, that was for sure, and given that he wasn't fucking her, she doubted he would care much about whatever infection was breeding down there in her moist nether regions.

Unless he was planning on selling her.

Was that what this was?

Some sex slavery thing?

Was he keeping her in that room, fed and relatively clean because a buyer was going to come and inspect her at some point in the near future?

No.

He had been in that house to kill her father, not to abduct her.

She had simply been in the wrong place at the wrong time.

But why not kill her too?

And why kill him?

These were questions that she couldn't answer, questions that kept bouncing around within her mind, dominating her thoughts.

The smell of something burning floated up into the room, shifting her focus.

It was almost dinnertime, which meant he would be releasing her to use the bathroom and then eat, all before locking her back up and then, if it was one of those nights, heading out until morning to wherever it was he went. A night job perhaps. Something suited for the disfigured freak that he was.

She needed to compose herself and get ready.

Though no opportunity for escape had ever presented itself during these brief moments of freedom from the strait-jacket, she knew it was important to stay focused during them and keep her eyes peeled on the chance that he would make a mistake. One slip-up on his part and she could be free, her body pushing past him and bolting through the door.

And then what?

She had no idea what lay beyond the house, but figured there had to be a road of some kind out there. After all, he had driven her all the way up to the house itself, the time between being pulled from the trunk and carried inside a minute at most, so there would be a path toward civilization if she could get free.

But how far away was it?

And what if he caught her before she could reach it?

GRAMMA MATILDA HAD A NICELY SEASONED cast-iron skillet that did nothing to improve upon Josiah's cooking talents, or lack thereof. It didn't matter how much he studied the food websites, YouTube videos, or whatever instructions he managed to pull from the cloudy mind of the wrinkled woman, anything he tried to cook ended up looking like the charred remains of a napalmed gook.

Frustration followed.

Rage too.

So much wasted time and effort.

Not to mention the life of a bird.

He didn't even know why he bothered with cooking.

Boredom might have been a part of it.

A desire for normality another.

You'll never be normal, the Father had told him.

He had a purpose in life, one that was divinely inspired.

Embracing it was his only option.

Until he did that, his life would always feel off—like he was straddling a fence, one that he occasionally would step off of but then jump back onto a few seconds later.

He needed to make a decision.

The Decision.

Nothing could progress until he did.

But...

He wanted an answer about Joel's daughter.

She was one of the reasons he was still on the fence.

He didn't tell the Father this.

He didn't dare.

But he had an idea that the Father knew and that it was one of the reasons he hadn't given him any instructions on what to do with her. The Father wanted to know that he could resist his earthly desires and commit fully to the Lord. The Father wanted to know that his focus would be unbroken.

Once he committed, the Father would then reveal what the girl's purpose was and Josiah would have no choice but to comply.

He won't let me have her.

Josiah somehow knew this even though it hadn't been conveyed to him, disappointment flooding his body as he scraped the ruined chicken into the yard, several barnyard cats watching with interest but refusing to approach until he was gone.

He stepped back inside, hand setting the cast-iron skillet back onto the stove, thoughts on if he should even bother with scraping the burnt crud from within echoing in his mind.

Maybe getting rid of the skillet would help put an end to his cooking temptations, thus allowing him to focus on things that were more important.

Maybe—

The sound of brakes that needed some serious work caught his attention as a vehicle came to a halt in the turnabout out front.

He sighed, not even needing to look out the window to know that it was Blake, and that he had come to scold him about the chicken.

SOMETHING WAS OFF. Mel had smelled the cooking and heard the frustration of whatever had gone wrong, but then the typical stairway ascent as the big man with the scars brought her one of those military pouch meals that he seemed to have in endless supply did not follow.

Voices!

She couldn't make out what was being said, but there certainly was a conversation taking place, one that had a different ring to it than previous conversations that had unfolded below.

Indecision gripped her.

Should she try to call attention to herself?

She could not scream for help, but that didn't mean she couldn't make some sort of noise that would alert whoever was down there to her presence.

The question was, did they already know she was up there and would calling attention to herself simply cause some form of punishment to unfold?

I have to try.

If she didn't...

"YOU PROMISED ME YOU WOULD STOP," Blake said while standing in the front hallway, arms crossed.

Josiah shrugged.

"You can't keep doing this," he continued. "If you do, he's going to press charges, and then I'll have no choice but to bring you in for theft."

"It's just a chicken," Josiah said.

"One that didn't belong to you."

Josiah shrugged again.

"Look, you wouldn't walk into a grocery store and take a frozen chicken from their cooler, would you?"

"No."

"Then why do you keep walking onto Colin's farm and taking them?"

"It's different."

"It's not different. It's the exact same thing. Worse actually. A grocery store can take the loss. Colin can't."

Josiah didn't reply.

Blake waited several seconds and then said, "Do you need help?"

"Help?"

"With getting food and making meals. We can get a group together. It wouldn't take much. People will help if you need it. Especially around here. We appreciate your sacrifice. Even Colin. His wife will probably fry a chicken for you. All you have to do is say the words."

Josiah shook his head.

Blake stared at him, his eyes obviously trying to avoid the scars but having a difficult time with it.

"Anything else?" Josiah asked.

"Joe, I'm serious about this. I hope you realize that. If you take another chicken or anything else from—"

A crash upstairs cut him off.

Blake's eyes went wide. "What was that?" he asked.

"Just one of the windows slamming shut," Josiah said. "Rollers are bad."

"That was not a window," Blake said.

Another crash.

Josiah grabbed Blake and slammed him into the wall as hard as he could, plaster shattering, his revolver falling to the ground.

"Joe?" Blake questioned, voice heavy.

Josiah shifted his hands to the man's throat and squeezed, his fingers feeling the panicked pulses as Blake tried to keep his airway open.

It was no use.

MEL SAT ON THE BED, trembling, the struggles from down below having ended several seconds earlier. Nothing but silence followed, one that seemed to encase her as if it were an additional restraint upon her body.

A groan as weight settled upon a wooden step echoed up.

And then another.

No!

It was him, the big man with the scars.

Only he could create such heartache by simply taking a step upon the stairs.

Knocking over the nightstand had been a mistake, one that she was now going to suffer for.

Another step.

Tears began to fall once again, each step making them more and more pronounced.

Snot joined the tears, bubbles of it oozing from her nostrils as she struggled to breathe.

Another step.

And then a voice from down below shouted something.

The steps stopped.

More shouts, the word *rats* reaching her ears.

"*No, no, it's all right!*" the man with the scars shouted.

The shouts continued, terror evident in the elderly voice.

And then the front door opened and slammed.

"*No! Stop!*"

Confusion momentarily usurped Mel's fear.

Steps groaned once again, but this time it was due to the heavy thuds as the man turned and headed back down.

And then the sound of the door opening and closing once again echoed up.

Silence followed.

Mel had no idea what was going on, but whatever it was, she was thankful for the momentary reprieve it had granted her. Unfortunately, she knew it would only be a matter of time before he returned. A matter of time before he came up the stairs, anger about what she had done dominating.

But maybe that would be better than whatever else it was he had planned for her.

Or didn't have planned.

Just having something happen rather than staying in the bed, straightjacketed, gagged, being fed and cleaned from time to time might be good.

Or it might not.

THREE

THOUGH SHE HAD no way of knowing for sure, Mel felt that at least an hour had passed since the commotion down on the first floor had unfolded, the silence of the house finally broken when the sounds of the front door opening and shutting echoed up to her, followed by weighted steps going back and forth.

The man with the scars was back.

Mel had tried to free herself during this period of time, the flipped-over nightstand having offered a semi-sharp edge to work with in cutting open the straitjacket.

She failed.

The canvas was too thick to puncture or tear, and the straps too well buckled for her to work them open.

It was hopeless.

Even worse, the burning in her crotch had grown worse from all the activity, the strap between her legs acting like an unrelenting torture device. Humiliation would soon follow, the urge to release her bladder growing more and more pressing by the minute, her body having grown accustomed to her dinner releases.

Would he come up and let her use the bathroom?

Normally he would, but after his return he seemed occupied by something downstairs, and then after a while, the front door opened and closed again.

She had no idea where he was going and was torn between hoping it was one of his long nightly disappearances versus a simple stroll that would find him returning soon so he could free her to use the bathroom.

Seconds turned to minutes, which accumulated.

He did not return.

She waited, her mind trying to think of anything but her bladder and the need that was growing more and more desperate, the burning sensation not helping at all. In fact, it seemed to make things worse.

He still did not return.

And whoever else was in the house was not making any sounds, and even if they had been, they never ever came up to where she was located.

Why?

Are they locked up themselves?

Is he slowly but surely filling each room of the house with captives?

No answers arrived, and even if they had, they wouldn't have made a difference.

All that mattered was trying to get free. After that, she could focus on what was beyond the room and if there were any others being held captive.

Only getting free didn't seem possible.

Adding to the horror, she was going to wet herself soon.

Even if he suddenly came back and started to free her so that she could use the bathroom, it would be no use.

The pressure was too much, especially with the burning that was overwhelming the area.

She had to let it out.

Fresh tears began to fall, the tiny bit of liquid that rolled down her cheeks nothing compared to the onslaught that sprayed against the strap and then ran down her legs. She stood against the wall during the humiliating release, legs spread, her hope being that none of the piss would get on the long skirt he had put her in, one whose waistband was pulled up around the lower portion of the straitjacket.

JOSIAH NEEDED to speak with the Father but couldn't see him because he was taking part in an after-dinner group, which Josiah wasn't allowed to attend.

"*You make everyone uncomfortable,*" Joel had told him several weeks earlier, prior to a meeting.

It was his size that did it, and the scars, most of them from the war, others from his acts of purification.

Others in his situation might grow resentful of such shunning, but Josiah had become used to it, given that it was a staple of his existence. All his life people had been wary of him. It didn't matter what the setting or activity was, within a day or two of his participation, a barrier would go up between him and the others. Even in the military this had been the case, though unlike other groups he had tried to be a part of, they hadn't suggested he throw in the towel and find something else to occupy his time. Instead, they had maneuvered him into a position where his oddities could be utilized and his mental isolation beneficial—up until the *incident*.

But that was okay.

Without the incident, he never would have ended up here and met the Father, and without meeting the Father, he would never have come to realize his true purpose in life.

He was a part of God's plan, and not a minuscule speck in a collection of specks that were maneuvered around as a whole without much care. Nope. He had an individual purpose, one that God had specifically chosen him for, which meant that he himself was known by God. Few in the history of existence were honored with such a role. In fact, it was so rare that even aspiring to such a position was met with scorn from the masses. And those who did achieve such a position were often viewed as crazy and dangerous, their lives cut short as they were martyred for their belief and devotion.

Would the same happen to him?

To the Father?

The question hung heavy in his mind and once again made him wonder why God would so often allow His chosen ones to be butchered. If they had a purpose and were part of the plan, then why not let them fulfill that purpose and plan?

There are elements we still do not understand, the Father had told him.

At the time, Josiah had nodded as if that had answered the question, even though it had not. Instead, it made him realize that asking such questions of the Father was not going to bring about answers. And that was okay. It was not his job to understand those aspects of the Lord. He only needed to focus on his purpose. He would fulfill his role while the Father fulfilled his, and together they would be instrumental in furthering God's plan. Whether they would be the final steps that helped complete the plan was a mystery, but given how horrible the world had become, and the signs, it was not beyond the realm of possibility.

Excitement blossomed at the thought but then faded as he remembered why he had shown up unannounced.

He had killed a county deputy, all because the girl had drawn attention to herself.

He needed to know what to do.

Not about the deputy, though he did need to let the Father

know about that just in case it changed things, but about what to do with the girl because her presence was jeopardizing things. The longer he kept her up in the room, the riskier it became. She was like a doorway for the enemy, one that they might eventually use in an attempt to jeopardize God's plan.

I should have taken care of her at Joel's place.

It would have been so simple, her body no match for his as he put his hands around her throat and squeezed, body straddling hers, hands occasionally loosening to let air through so as to prolong the experience.

And then he would have put her in the trunk and eventually disposed of her out in the fields.

Would the Father have known?

Would God have told him?

Or would something else have happened?

Would his enjoyment of the moment make him oblivious to a danger that was looming, one that would have found its way into the room and ruined things?

He touched the side of his face while contemplating this, memories of Afghanistan flowing.

Memories of the girl.

Her eyes were always the first thing that returned to him, the tiny blue orbs looking like diamonds as they tracked his approach within the hut.

And then her skin.

It had been soft. Almost like silk. The tears that ran down it looking as if they belonged in one of those moisturizer commercials back in the States.

She shivered beneath his fingers, his mind not even aware of having taken off his gloves so that he could wipe away her tears, a gentle statement on how it was going to be okay leaving his lips.

"Shhh," he continued, his left hand joining his right.

A hand touched his shoulder, jerking him from the memory, his own hand nearly grabbing the wrist and breaking it before he remembered where he was.

Terror was present on the young man's face, his features looking far too boyish for the position he carried, the uniform, which would have been intimidating on anyone else, almost comical in this situation.

"I'm sorry, sir, you can't be here," the young man said.

"What?" Josiah said, blinking the last of the memory away. "No, I'm waiting to see—"

"Sir, please."

"Do you know who I am?" Josiah asked.

It was obvious he didn't.

"I need to speak with the—"

Another uniform loomed nearby, this one on a figure that looked far more intimidating than the boy who stood before him.

He wasn't going to get to see the Father that evening.

That much was clear.

This boy and his companion hovering nearby had no idea who he was, which was one of the downsides to him always interacting one-on-one with the Father. Others didn't realize his significance, and then misunderstandings like this could develop.

Or did they know who he was?

Had Joel poisoned everyone?

Or maybe the Father didn't want to see him and had sent them?

Would the Father have done that to him even though Josiah had sent a message to him through one of his orderlies that they needed to talk?

Was the urgency that he had expressed not properly conveyed?

Or had the orderly not even passed it on?

Had it been intercepted?

Or was the Father worried about them drawing too much attention to themselves, the situation with Joel still fresh in his mind?

No answers were available.

None would be until he could speak with the Father.

"Sir," the boy said, hand returning to his shoulder.

"I'm going," Josiah said, standing.

The walls of the compound spun, the sudden rush of blood nearly too much for him.

And then it passed.

How long had he been sitting?

A partial answer to that arrived as he stepped outside and saw that the sun had nearly set, the moon starting to take its position in the darkening sky.

This wasn't good.

He had lost time again.

Not much, but enough for it to be of concern, especially since the body of the deputy was still in the front room of the house, his county-issued cruiser in the turnabout.

Why had he come here before addressing that?

What was wrong with him?

He didn't need the Father to advise him on how to handle a body.

Handling such situations was his job, his purpose, so that the Father could keep himself pure.

The questions on the girl could wait.

Whatever threat she posed was nothing compared to that of a cooling body in the house he was temporarily living in while getting the sanctuary ready, the county cruiser like a beacon that shouted, "*Something happened here!*"

Frustrated with himself for the lapse and knowing he would have to atone for it once everything was settled, he got into Gramma Matilda's car and started back toward the farm, his hope being that given the isolation of the place, no one had yet noticed Blake's vehicle parked out front. If they had...

Nothing followed.

He had no idea what would happen.

He had no contingency plan for such a situation.

It was another lapse, one that he couldn't believe he had allowed to take root.

You've been too dependent on the instructions of the Father, a voice that wasn't his own said within his mind.

God? he asked.

Nothing followed.

THE NEIGHBOR with the chickens was going to be a problem. Josiah realized this as he headed back toward the farm.

One word from him and the sheriff would know what it was Blake had been up to in the hours before his disappearance. Once that happened...

Josiah didn't even want to go any further with those thoughts.

The consequences were too horrible.

The neighbor needed to be eliminated.

It was the only option—the only way to ensure that he would be able to continue with God's plan.

The wife and daughter...

Josiah had spent quite a bit of time thinking about the two women during the early days of his life on the farm, his eyes having first spotted the daughter while out wandering the fields. She was pretty, the type of girl who probably drove the boys nuts at school, the type who could get them to do whatever she asked, the type who would never have given him much thought back when he had been a teen.

The mother was fat.

She also seemed like a bitch, the type of woman who did not abide by her husband's wishes and tried to dominate the household. He knew this because he had watched through his binoculars as she railed at her husband while *he* hung up the laundry on a clothesline, her arms flailing, fat jiggling. It had been a disgusting sight, both because of how gross she was and because it totally upset the natural household order that God had wanted for mankind.

Women like that will have a hard time once the Lord returns to establish His kingdom, the Father had told him after Josiah had shared what he had witnessed. *Reeducation camps will likely have to be set up to teach them how to be proper wives that respect their husbands.*

Such camps and the kingdom were still a long ways off, and given the current threat the family posed, this disrespectful wife would not live long enough to get a second chance at being a proper wife.

But such was the way of the world.

Many would die before the kingdom was established.

He himself might not even live to see it, though he would be instrumental in helping to bring about its establishment, which was exciting.

Now the question was, which issue needed to be addressed first: the county cruiser or the family?

Several seconds ticked by without an answer.

And then a minute.

Two minutes.

Three minutes.

Concern began to build.

He didn't know what to do.

Anxiety appeared.

And then the voice returned, one that pretty much told him he needed to rid himself of the deputy's county cruiser first, and then deal with the family on his return from that.

Once again, he couldn't help but wonder if God was speaking to him.

If so, why now?

This question did not receive an answer, but that was okay.

The reason for the timing was not important.

All that mattered was that the voice had given him instructions, ones that made sense and could be followed.

THE ROOM SMELLED LIKE PISS.

Her piss.

It hung heavy in the air, a constant reminder of the humiliation she had been forced to endure.

Guilt was present as well.

And anger.

And fear.

She was a mess.

Physically and mentally.

Tears stained her face, along with sweat that had built up during her frantic escape attempts, the heavy canvas of the straitjacket making her feel as if she was being marinated in her own filth.

She wanted to get out.

She needed to get out.

But nothing she did even gave her a glimmer of hope.

The canvas of the straitjacket was too tough, and the straps too tight. She could not tear it, nor shake it loose. Attempting to get free of it was useless. All it did was wear her out.

She bucked on the bed in frustration, the entire frame bouncing off the wooden floor and coming back down with a serious crash.

Careful! her crazed mind warned. *Don't want to break another bed.*

An audible laugh tried to escape her mouth, the sound crashing into the gag.

Her friend Amy had gotten a spanking for that when they were kids. With a wooden spoon. Mel hearing the sounds of the strikes and the cries as she sat outside the house. All because Mel had given one final defiant jump on the bed after Amy's mother had told them to stop. She had not intended to actually break the bed, but apparently all the prior jumps had done some damage, and her one final jump had been the straw that broke the camel's back, Amy's mother obviously hearing the destruction because she charged back into the room within seconds, right hand grabbing Amy's arm.

Mel had tried to tell Amy's mom that it had been her, but the bitch wouldn't listen as she dragged Amy into the kitchen and retrieved the wooden spoon from a drawer. She had then told Mel to go home and that she was banned from the house.

The spankings had quickly followed, Mel sitting outside the house in tears as her friend was beaten, wondering if she should tell her own parents about the punishment, but fearful that if she did, she might get in trouble herself.

In the end, she had never said a word.

And Amy had refused to talk to her after that, the friendship quickly crumbling.

All because of that one final bounce.

Could she replicate the destructive act?

How many bounces would it take to break this one?

And afterward, would she be able to escape, or would she still be stuck and eventually punished when the big man with the scars came home?

Would he use a wooden spoon?

The thought brought about another laugh, the gag once again not letting it through.

And then she bucked her body into a bounce.

Wood groaned.

Another bounce.

And another.

She stood up and jumped as high as she could, legs folding so that she could land on her knees.

Wood splintered.

Whoops! I did it again.

Downstairs the front door opened.

Shit.

He was back.

She looked at the bed and realized that even if he came up, he would not notice anything. On the surface, the bed looked fine. It actually felt fine too while on it. But something had broken. And if one part of the bed could break, others could as well, which meant it might be possible to free the chain.

"RATS!" Gramma Matilda shouted. "Upstairs. Rats everywhere!"

"Shhhh," Josiah said. "It's okay. There're no rats."

"Rats! Rats!" Her eyes were crazed.

He simply smiled and then said, "I have to go out again, so let's get you into—"

"Rats!"

He shook his head. It was no use. Her mind was stuck. "Come on, let me get you back into bed."

"Upstairs. Rats. I hear them. Everywhere."

It clicked.

The girl.

He had gotten so focused on Blake and needing to speak to the Father that he had completely forgotten about feeding her and letting her use the bathroom.

It's her own fault.

If she hadn't made that crashing sound...

Then again, if she wet herself (or worse), he would have to be the one to clean up, so who was really being punished?

Get rid of the deputy and the cruiser.

Now!

Everything else could wait.

FOUR

DRIVING the county cruiser while not in a uniform was risky, but even if Blake hadn't soiled himself, Josiah's size would have made it impossible to don his clothing. Even wearing the tan shirt with the county patch and American flag so that he looked the part when viewed through the window was not possible. Blake was an average-sized man; Josiah was not. Attempting to put his arms through the sleeves would have ripped open the back.

Fortunately, the sun had finished its descent and darkness had taken hold, so seeing into the cruiser while he was driving was next to impossible without putting one's face against the glass. Plus, he was driving along streets that were rarely used during the day, let alone at night, so chances were good that he would not even come across anyone while making the journey to the banks of the Meramec River.

Will it work?

No answer followed.

Nor did a better idea.

The cruiser would be found. It didn't matter what he did with it. Once a deputy failed to show up for a shift, the county would try to find him, and the longer they went without finding him, the more they would focus on mapping out what exactly he did after leaving the county headquarters for the day. By putting the cruiser near the river, Josiah would make it so they not only found it quickly, but would also have a plausible scenario on what might have happened to him.

Some might grow suspicious of the setup, but others would accept that he had had a tragic accident and move on, the level of scrutiny far less than it would have been if he and his cruiser had simply vanished. After all, people fell in the river all the time. Not just kids, but adults too. Drinking was usually involved, but other times it wasn't. Water was dangerous. Especially when high and moving fast from the summer deluges that had pummeled the northern part of the state. Rocks were also present, the river having done quite a bit during its post-flood existence to carve out a path in the land. All it took was one jarring hit against one of the protruding edges and a person who might have been a good swimmer in any other situation would find themselves struggling to stay afloat and eventually drown. Blake would go down as one of those statistics.

It wasn't a perfect plan, but it was the best he could come up with during the time allowed.

Shouldn't have taken that chicken.

Past experience had told him he wouldn't have been able to fry it up properly and that it would likely go to waste, but after seeing it roaming around while in the brush hoping to get another glimpse of the farmer's daughter, the urge had become too strong and he could not resist. Envisioning a platter of perfectly fried chicken the way Gramma Matilda had made it when he was a kid had also played a part, his longing to enjoy such a meal too much for him to not give it another try.

And now you have all this to deal with.

Wise up!

Guilt arrived.

He had put God's plan in jeopardy, all because he had wanted some fried chicken.

No.

Because you wanted to watch the girl and fantasize.

Josiah could not deny this.

Staying pure was difficult, especially with the girl chained to the bed upstairs, the urge to undo the crotch strap and climb atop her growing with each passing day. And given her proximity, fantasizing while in the house itself was not a viable option because it could easily go from fantasy to reality.

Sometimes the flame was enough to suppress the urges.

Sometimes it wasn't.

Sometimes he needed to venture out into the fields and relieve himself.

Today had been one of those days.

What's done is done, he said to himself.

All he could do now was fix the mess his urges had created and move on.

No other option was present.

No choice.

Fix things and move on.

No.

Fix things, cleanse yourself, and then move on.

His actions required an atonement, one that would be more intense and severe than simply holding the flame to his flesh, one that would cleanse his body, mind, and soul.

He shivered at the thought but also relished it because it would realign himself with the Lord and His purpose.

It would—

Something bolted out from the field, its massive body turning toward the cruiser, its eyes glowing red in the light and bearing down on him.

Josiah hit the brakes, the tires squealing as they struggled to engage, the vehicle fishtailing along the pockmarked pavement.

The beast stood its ground for several seconds, steam rising from its nostrils while its red eyes continued glaring at Josiah, before it turned and disappeared into the field, heading toward the river.

Heart racing and his knuckles white as they gripped the wheel, Josiah stared at the emptiness where the beast had stood, horror at what had nearly happened threatening to overwhelm him.

Satan.

He had sent the beast to try to stop him, to muck things up so that he would not succeed in continuing with the Lord's plan.

No doubt about it.

What had resembled a large deer had really been a hellspawn sent up from the fiery depths, one that had just barely failed in its mission.

If he had not stopped in time...

Josiah didn't even want to continue the thought.

The beast had failed, and that was all that mattered.

But it might try again.

Or something else would be sent, something even more powerful.

He took a deep breath and tried to focus.

The beast may have failed, but that didn't mean he was in the clear. He had a lot of work to do that evening, work that would not get done if he simply sat there in the middle of the dark street, contemplating things.

No.

He needed to act.

Taking his foot from the brake and easing the grip his fingers had on the wheel, Josiah got the vehicle back into the correct lane of travel and continued down the road to the spot where he planned on staging the accidental drowning death of Blake.

BREAKING the bed frame proved more difficult than Mel had anticipated, her bounces upon the mattress causing things to creak and splinter, but not snap or shatter. Making things worse, she had no idea where exactly the chain was connected, her inability to move the mattress from where it was cradled within the wooden frame preventing her from knowing where she should focus her destructive efforts.

She needed her hands.

She needed to be able to lift the mattress up so she could see where the chain was connected and where the closest weak point was.

She needed—

Movement!

She heard it on the stairs.

It was a soft groan as someone planted a foot upon a step, someone who obviously was not the big man with the scars.

The other.

The one she had never seen before.

Prisoner? Accomplice? She did not know, but whoever they were, they were now on the stairs.

Mel waited.

Another gentle groan.

And then another.

They were coming up.

But why?

Was it because of the noise she was making?

No other possibility seemed plausible.

She had never before bounced like this while in the house, and they had never before come up the stairs.

But why not?

Were the stairs usually blocked off to them?

Or was this other person a prisoner that had managed to free themselves and now was coming up to help?

Another step.

Mel gave a mental shake of her head, the latter possibility not seeming correct.

Something else was happening, something she wouldn't be able to decipher from just sitting on the mattress thinking.

Another step, this one followed by what sounded like a word being muttered, but one she could not understand.

Mel shook her head and went back to focusing on the bed, a decision to get down on the floor and peer under it to see what type of damage she was causing unfolding.

"*Ratsss.*"

Mel spun toward the door, the voice having slithered up from the stairs.

Another step groaned.

"*Rats. Rats. Rats.*"

What the fuck?

The voice sounded so frail that a gust of wind could have easily shattered it, yet it also carried a menace to it, one that sent a shiver down her spine.

And the sounds of ascent had changed. They were no longer taking one step at a time. Instead, there was a rustling type of sound and the occasional solid *thunk* noise, all of it accompanied by the chanting.

Mel went to the doorway, the chain giving her just enough slack so that she could angle herself to peer down the hallway and glimpse the top of the stairway.

No one was visible yet, though the sounds as they struggled up made it seem like they were getting close.

"*Rathssss! Rathssss!*"

A hand appeared, bony fingers trying to find something to grab hold of at the top of the stairway.

Mel gasped against the gag.

They were crawling up the stairs.

The hand found the edge and secured leverage for the rest of the struggling body, gray hair appearing as an old withered face crested the wooden step, strained wrinkles dominating her pinched features.

Milky white eyes glared her way.

She wasn't blind, but obviously could not see very well.

A groan echoed and then a second hand swung up over her head and came down hard on the top of the landing with a heavy *thunk*.

A rolling pin?

The old lady had crawled up the steps with a rolling pin.

Why?

"*Rats!*" the old woman hissed toward Mel, milky white eyes locking onto her before slamming the rolling pin into the floor.

Oh shit.

Mel tried to grab the door so she could close it, but it was beyond her reach.

Thunk!

Mel strained against the chain, but the bed would not budge, her feet unable to get the leverage she needed to close the distance between herself and the door.

"*Rats.*"

Mel turned back.

The old lady had completed her journey up the steps and now was sprawled upon the floor, milky white eyes still staring her way, lungs heaving as she struggled to recover her breath.

And then she began to stand.

JOSIAH DIDN'T DUMP Blake into the river. He didn't even bring the body, which was still in the front room of the house.

Nope. This journey was simply about positioning the cruiser so that the focus was the river and the possibility of Blake having fallen in. The body itself would be disposed of in the fields behind the farm where, God willing, it would never be found. Such was the only way to keep the falsehood of the river death alive. If he actually dumped the body in the river, it would eventually be found, and once that happened, it would be clear to even the most inept medical examiner that his death had come long before he had been put into the water and that all the damage suffered while in the river was postmortem.

The hellspawn did not show itself while he positioned the vehicle.

He had expected it to—almost wanted it to so he could get a better look at it—but it hadn't.

Josiah wasn't sure what this meant, but knew it was far from positive.

It having failed while on the road was good, of that there was no question, but the fact that it had been sent in the first place was a sign that Satan was actively working against him.

Knowing this was unsettling.

He knew the forces of evil were out there and that Heaven and Hell were locked in a perpetual battle for dominance over mankind, but up until now he had never been specifically targeted within the great battle—that he knew of.

And the fact that it had been a hellspawn that was sent rather than a human agent only added to the significance. It also reinstated the importance of what he was doing. After all, Satan would not have taken the time to single him out if his actions weren't worrisome to the forces of evil. Had he simply been an unimportant speck among Christ's warriors, he would have been left alone to continue in the war against the equally unimportant human warriors of Satan's army. But no, he had been specifically targeted.

I need to tell the Father.

Not only did this attack justify what it was they were working toward, it also signaled a shift in how far the enemy was willing to go in the war, one that could mean the end was closer than they had anticipated.

What this meant, Josiah did not know, but he knew it was significant and something the Father would need to find out about as soon as possible.

"RATS!" the old woman hissed, rolling pin raised, body wobbling as she took tiny steps toward Mel, the milky white eyes locked on her in a way that was almost hypnotic. "Rats! Rats!"

Mel backed into the room, feet nearly tripping over the chain as the slack pooled behind her.

"Rats!"

Mel tried to protest, but no words could make it through the gag.

It took several seconds, but eventually the woman scurried her way into the doorway, head slowly swiveling as she tried to see into the room.

Mel didn't move and tried not to breathe.

The old woman waited nearly a minute before stepping in, rolling pin raised and ready. Her exhaustion was evident. Coming up the stairs had completely drained her, yet a determination was present as well. She was going to kill the rats.

The old woman sniffed the air, face shriveling with a wince.

She then turned toward the corner where Mel had peed.

A mumbled word left her cracked lips.

This time it didn't sound like *rats*.

It was something else, something that Mel had not understood.

Not that it would have mattered if she had. She couldn't respond. She couldn't protest. All she could do was wait, watch, and try to stay out of the old lady's swinging range.

Does she think I'm a rat?

How far gone was she?

The old lady turned toward her, an odd smile on her face.

Could she smell the piss?

Or just her in general, given how long she had been up here sweating into the straitjacket?

The old lady stepped toward her.

She didn't smell very good herself, a mix of piss, shit, and old person rot.

Both of them needed a bath.

Another step.

She was almost within swinging reach.

Mel didn't know what to do.

If she moved, the chain might startle the old lady and make her swing, but then again, if she was already confused to the point of thinking Mel might be a rat, she would likely swing anyway once she was within reach.

Another step.

Mel backed up.

"Rats!" the old lady shouted.

Mel hit the edge of the bed, the wooden frame knocking her legs out from under her, the mattress absorbing her fall while also providing her with a spring to bounce herself around to the opposite side, her movement momentarily halted as something snagged the chain.

She turned and watched as the old lady crumpled to the floor beyond the bed, a *thunk* and then an odd gasp leaving her lips.

A nasty gurgle sound followed.

Mel hesitated for several seconds and then started around

the bed, the chain giving a bit of resistance as she moved, but not to the point of it halting her.

A new smell hit the air, one that carried a strong fecal element to it.

Mel had a feeling she knew what she was going to find.

JOSIAH STARED at the farmhouse for a long time, his body exhausted after the long trek from the river. His mind, on the other hand, struggled to maintain its calm amid the excitement that was building within. This was the reason he was staring. He didn't want to rush things. He didn't want a repeat of what had happened when he went in to kill Joel. He didn't want to be caught off guard by something unexpected.

In the distance, coyotes yipped.

A thought arrived.

If the farmer thought his chickens were in danger from a coyote, he might come outside and make an easy target. After all, coyotes were fearful creatures and would likely flee if he came out and made some noise, whereas if the farmer heard someone in his own home, he would probably address the situation more defensively and with a gun.

Actually, a gun might come into play either way, but with a coyote he would probably simply fire a shot into the air since that would be just as effective as trying to aim in the dark and hitting one.

Decision made, Josiah moved into the back area of the farm toward where the chickens were kept.

THE OLD LADY WAS DEAD, her head having smashed against the corner of the overturned nightstand after her ankle had gotten snared by a loop of chain as Mel rolled across the bed. It was a horrific sight, mostly because her milky white eyes were wide open, as was her mouth, both looking surprised.

My fault.

No.

Yes.

The old lady had heard the sounds she was making and went up to investigate, her confused mind unable to figure out what it was she was hearing and imprinting the idea of rats upon it to understand.

But why a rolling pin?

Had she used one in the past to kill rats?

The image of such a thing would have been amusing if it wasn't so horrific.

She shook her head and sat on the edge of the bed, exhaustion getting the better of her.

All that bouncing and she had accomplished absolutely nothing.

And now she had an old dead lady as a companion, one who had soiled herself.

She could have killed you.

One smash against the side of the head with the rolling pin could have done it.

Mel touched the rolling pin with her foot while contemplating this, her toes moving it back and forth a bit along the floorboards.

No, the old lady wouldn't have been able to kill her, not unless she was able to summon a huge burst of strength when making a swing, and given how exhausted she had seemed after coming up the steps, managing such a thing seemed beyond the realm of possibility.

The man on the other hand...he could easily kill her with the rolling pin.

Shit, he just might after seeing this.

Depending on how close the two were, he might grab the rolling pin and smash her brains out in a fit of rage.

A few weeks earlier, imagining such a thing would have horrified her, but now it didn't really faze her. If he smashed her brains out, this would all be over. It wasn't the outcome she hoped for, but it was an outcome, one that would be better than some of the others her mind had been allowed to envision while chained up in the room.

This thought once again led her to wondering why.

Why was she here?

Why had he killed her dad?

WHY... WHY... WHY...

Her toes continued to play with the rolling pin as her mind asked the questions, the sounds of it rolling back and forth the only replies she got, and they weren't worth anything.

FIVE

MEL ZONED out for a bit while toying with the rolling pin, her mind drifting into a daze while she sat on the bed, body still pretzeled into the straitjacket, mouth stretched by the gag device, groin burning with whatever infection had taken root in the damaged flesh.

She wasn't going to be breaking free.

Not from this bed.

It was too solid.

Her bounces had accomplished nothing beyond getting the old lady killed, something that might lead to her own death once the man returned.

This didn't bother her all that much.

Not knowing the why of everything did.

What had her dad done to invite this man's rage?

Why had he been targeted?

No reasons seemed plausible.

All her dad did was work and watch TV.

It didn't make any sense, unless of course her mother had been behind it.

And maybe that was why she was being kept prisoner.

Maybe the big man with the scars had realized he could ransom her back.

Or maybe her mother had decided to let the man teach her some sort of convoluted lesson, one that involved keeping her chained up in this room for a month or two so that when she did eventually go back home, she would have a different appreciation for what she had with her mom.

No.

Mel couldn't say why her dad had been killed and she kidnapped, but she did know her mom wasn't behind it.

Something else was going on.

Something she would probably never be able to understand.

Not unless she was able to turn the tables on the man and make him talk, though given all the scars he had, she doubted doing that would be possible.

Plus, how could she turn the tables on him?

Even during the moments when he freed her so she could use the bathroom and eat, there was no way for her to overpower him. She knew this because she had tried. Several times. All to no avail.

And tripping him with the chain so that he cracked open his head wouldn't work.

No.

The only way she would be able to turn the tables on him was if she had a weapon, one that she could use during the moments he freed her from the jacket, one that he would not expect and not be able to defend against right away.

But she didn't have a weapon.

Unless...

She stopped toying with the rolling pin and looked at it.

Would it work as a weapon?

Would smashing it into the side of the big man's head be

enough to knock him senseless so that she could bring it down over and over again until his brains oozed out?

Or at least knock him senseless so she could get away?

GETTING the chickens to make noise was not easy, and in the end Josiah had to pull two of the sleeping birds from the roost, carry them all the way to the back of the house, and break their legs to get them squawking.

Once he did that, he simply waited.

Two minutes later, a light appeared within an upstairs window, followed by another on the ground floor, and then finally one that was over the back door, this one partially illuminating the yard and porch area.

The farmer stepped out.

He didn't have a shotgun, but even if he had, it wouldn't have made a difference.

Josiah took him from behind, crushing his windpipe with a chokehold that he had learned at Fort Bragg and perfected in Kandahar, the black-turbaned towel-heads never even knowing what hit them.

Following that, Josiah dragged the farmer's lifeless body into the darkness of the yard and then went up to one of the back windows and peeked inside, the light within making it easy for him to see that no one had followed the farmer down the stairs.

In he went, excitement starting to build as he crossed the threshold.

He took a deep breath and calmed himself.

Best not to get too excited until he was sure all the threats within were eliminated, his combat experiences having taught him that the female half of humanity could be just as deadly as the male half.

Stairways were also a problem, memories of various raids in and around Baghdad coming back to him.

No one would be shooting at him or trying to time a grenade to explode while halfway down the steps, but if he was spotted while going up them, a call to the police could be made, which would complicate things—especially if a description went out over the airwaves.

That was the one problem with being over six feet tall.

Even without his scars, he stood out in a crowd, and with them he was pretty much impossible to miss.

Hence the reason Blake had known exactly who it was that had stolen a chicken the first time he had been spotted snatching one earlier that year.

Josiah shook his head and pushed the thoughts away so that he could focus on the task at hand.

He started up the stairs, the steps groaning with his weight.

If anyone heard it, they did not question it, and less than a minute later, he was on the landing, attention shifting toward the left since it had been a window on that side of the house that had brightened once the chickens started squawking.

The light was still on, the door to that room standing halfway open.

This could be tricky.

A scream from the fat wife could alert the daughter, who could then call the police, and while she hadn't seen him, and therefore wouldn't be able to give a description over the phone, his time with her would be cut short.

But maybe that would be for the best.

Less temptation that way.

He peered into the bedroom, eyes landing upon an empty bed.

Confusion turned to concern, his body quickly twisting back toward the hallway.

It was empty.

Four doors awaited.

One he guessed would be a bathroom, but from where he stood it was impossible to tell which one that would be. In fact, it was impossible to tell anything from just looking at them.

He would have to clear them one by one, his hope being to find and kill the fat wife before finding and savoring the daughter.

GETTING her toes around the handle of the rolling pin was easy; keeping them there, given its weight, was not.

It was a serious piece of baking equipment, one that had probably been crafted back when women themselves were viewed as a household appliance, one that could multitask throughout the various rooms if properly raised while the husband was out in the world making a living.

Disgust at the thought filled her mind.

She shook it away while getting a new grip on the handle, one foot pressing down on one side to elevate the other side a bit so that her big toe could get into a good position that would allow for a solid hold.

Handle secured, she once again lifted her leg, slowly at first so the weight could settle properly and then quicker so that she didn't have to support it for long, leg swinging over toward the bed.

Fuck!

She had not lifted it high enough, the edge of the mattress catching the last inch of the handle and knocking it from between her toes, her other leg swinging to try to knock it toward the bed but only managing to slam it into the edge of the mattress, which hurt.

It clattered to the floor and began to roll.

No!

She sprang from the bed, trying to stop it before it rolled out of reach, the stupid chain catching as she did and yanking her neck backward while also twisting the old woman's body, which caused an odd sound.

A new smell followed.

It joined the stench of piss that hovered in the air.

The rolling pin stalled itself out about three feet from the wall.

Relief flowed.

Mel could reach it.

At least she could once she untangled the chain from the dead woman's leg.

THE FIRST DOOR opened upon an empty bathroom.

The second door was locked.

The third as well.

The fourth was a linen closet.

Josiah stared at the two locked doors.

He had not been expecting this.

It was a problem.

Not the locks themselves, for he could easily get around them by kicking in the doors, but the noise that such action would produce.

USING HER TOES ONCE AGAIN, Mel unwound the chain from the old lady's leg and then went across the room to get the rolling pin, her journey back to the bed taking a bit of time as she slowly but surely nudged it into a position where she could sit down on the bed, grip it, and then lift it while slowly lowering herself backward to the mattress. Following that, she swung her leg, bringing the rolling pin into the center of the bed, and dropped it.

. . .

JOSIAH NEEDED to make a decision on what to do, his inaction while standing in the hallway staring at the two doors only fueling the chances that something else unexpected could arise. If he had a knife, things would be easier, but he didn't, so kicking in one door, cutting a throat, and then moving to the next was not an option, and crushing one's windpipe when they were springing up from sleep was not easy. Doable, yes, but awkward. Such an attack was always best from behind. When coming from the front, one had to find something to press the person up against, while being mindful of how vulnerable their own body became when face-to-face with a struggling person.

Right or left?

Give me a sign.

Please!

No sign followed.

He decided on the right since it was closer to the stairway, so if someone from the other room tried to flee, they had a few extra steps to take. Not many, but those steps could be the difference between life and death.

Taking a deep breath, Josiah kicked in the door and charged into the room, his eyes quickly settling upon the fat wife in a large bed of a large master bedroom, her sleep-filled eyes going from confusion to concern as she struggled to comprehend what had just happened.

An odd mask was attached to her face, its cords attached to a machine next to the bed.

A cry echoed, though not from the fat woman.

It came from the room next door, the explosion as the door was shattered having obviously startled the daughter awake.

Josiah hit the fat woman before she could sit up and use her size to try to hinder his attack, his fist shattering her jaw.

He then brought an elbow down onto her device-covered nose to crush it, thereby making it unlikely that she could call for help into a phone, her main focus trying to breathe through the pain of a broken jaw and nose, all while her own blood choked her.

He went back to the door.

The teen tried to dart by him toward the stairs, his hand snagging hold of her oversized T-shirt.

She spun toward him, fist swinging, and then yanked herself backward, the shirt tearing, her body hitting the banister and then tumbling right over it.

A brief cry followed by an ugly thump reached his ears.

Josiah hurried over to the banister.

She was still alive, but her body was badly twisted.

He heard a voice.

It seemed distant.

And then he saw it.

The teen had been holding a cell phone, one that she had dropped as he grabbed her.

The voice was that of an emergency dispatcher.

Josiah brought his foot down on it, crushing the phone and silencing the voice.

The clock was now ticking.

He turned his attention back to the fat woman in the bed.

She was still gurgling while struggling to get the broken device off her face.

He looked around and saw a desk lamp that had a wide, solid base, his right hand quickly grabbing it and bringing it down with all his strength, her hand trying to shield the blow, but failing. Several more followed in quick succession, the final one shattering her right eye socket, the organ within nothing but a pulpy mess while the left one was still intact, a lifeless gaze staring at him as blood oozed in and pooled between the open lids.

He dropped the lamp and went to the stairway, his eyes expecting to see the teen still crumpled on them.

She wasn't.

Panic arrived but was short-lived.

She had only managed to crawl into the main hallway, about eight feet from the bottom of the stairs, the movement obviously causing her considerable pain given that he could see the jagged edge of a broken leg bone protruding from her flesh. Her hips were also twisted sideways.

Grabbing hold of her hair, he dragged her into the kitchen where he started searching for a knife, all his desire to get atop her and thrust himself inside of her having fled, given that a call had been made and the police might be on their way.

She screamed while he did this, but without much force, her pain an obvious factor.

Blood dribbled from her mouth.

It was bright red, a sign that her lungs had likely been punctured.

Knife found, he cut her throat and then quickly did a search for something to start a fire with, the ticking clock making it so that he could not go around cleaning up any traces of himself.

AN ODD ANXIOUSNESS arrived once the rolling pin was tucked beneath the pillow, Mel almost feeling as if she were waiting to give some sort of speech in front of a class but had no idea when her name would be called.

One shot.

It was all she would get.

He would release her from the straitjacket, give her a moment to move her arms, and then wait as she used the bathroom and then ate whatever pouched meal he brought her.

At least, that was the normal order of things.

Given the old lady, she had no idea how things would unfold during the next visit to the room.

Once thing she did know: she wouldn't get any do-overs.

If she fumbled the rolling pin while grabbing it, or failed to hit him while swinging, or hit him without enough strength to cause damage, she would be fucked.

One shot.

No reset button.

At some point in the near future she would either find herself running down the street outside in an attempt to find help, or...

She had no idea what might happen if she failed.

Don't think about it!

Yeah right.

All she had were her thoughts.

She couldn't *not* think about it.

LIGHT from the house fire danced upon the horizon as Josiah crossed onto his grandmother's property, a feeling of relief at having rid himself of the threat that the farmer might link him to the disappearance of Blake overpowering the disappointment he felt at not being able to get atop the teen while his arms held her down against the mattress.

God stepped in.

That's why she fell down the stairs.

He knew the temptation would be too strong and would jeopardize the plan.

Things were coming to a head.

Of this, Josiah had no doubt.

The hellspawn earlier had been proof of this, and now the girl falling down the stairs helped cement it.

But what was the plan?

This was something he wanted to know more about, but the Father would not reveal it.

One thing he was sure about, the plan did not involve the coming eclipse.

He had been certain it would play a part back when he had first started working with the Father, but now, given that it was just days away, he doubted this was the case. Why the Father would not just tell him what the plan was, he didn't know, but that was the way it worked. Maybe it hadn't been fully revealed to him either. The Lord worked in mysterious ways.

An explosion echoed from the burning house behind him, the distance enough for him to not be concerned about it having any impact upon him or his grandmother's house.

He had no idea what the flames had caught, but whatever it was, it had been very combustible.

Memories of hearing explosions while in combat areas came back to him, as did the memories of how explosion-like noises had often caused him to jump or cry out when he had first come back to the States after recovering from his wounds.

Explosions and sudden noises no longer caused him problems.

Nothing really did.

The Father had helped him with this.

Being able to focus his mind on working for the Lord had rid him of his inner demons.

Well...most of them.

He still had the problem with wanting to have sex.

The Father had a solution for him, one that he continuously encouraged, but Josiah didn't want to go that route and had insisted he could get control of it himself.

But was that really the case?

Could he control it?

He wanted to say yes, the girl up in the bedroom of the

house was proof of this, but deep down inside he knew that it was only a matter of time before he gave in with her.

Thoughts on killing her before that happened had been considered, but such action would just be proof that he could not control himself and would need to take the steps the Father insisted upon.

Up ahead the house appeared.

The back porch light was on, as it always was when he needed to come home in the dark, but in addition to that, several lights on the ground floor were also lit, which wasn't right. He always made sure they were off before leaving.

Concern arrived.

Were the police there?

Had they known all along that Blake had planned on visiting him to talk about the chickens?

Had everything he had just done been for nothing?

MEL THOUGHT she heard an explosion off in the distance but couldn't be sure, and looking out the window did not help.

Nothing else followed, her body once against planting itself on the bed to wait.

What if he doesn't come back?

What if he got in some sort of accident and I am left to die?

What if...

On and on this went for an amount of time she could not measure, not with the sun having gone down.

And then the door downstairs opened.

Her body stiffened, her ears on call to see if she could tell who it was.

The steps were heavy.

Too heavy for anyone but the big man with the scars.

He had returned.

Her heartbeat quickened, her mind momentarily flashing

upon memories of coming face-to-face with various video game bosses that were difficult to defeat, her fingers knowing that one wrong move with the controller would mean defeat.

This time around her controller was the rolling pin.

She had one shot.

If she failed...

NO POLICE WERE WAITING to apprehend Josiah when he completed his journey to the house, the place—with the exception of the lights—as he had left it.

Still, something felt off.

He didn't know what, but a warning was echoing in the back of his mind.

He opened the front door.

Deputy Blake was where he had left him, body sprawled in the entryway, the stench of death hanging heavy in the air.

Stepping over him, Josiah headed down the hallway, eyes scanning things as he went.

Visually, nothing seemed amiss.

And then he saw the door to Gramma Matilda's room was standing open.

Had he forgotten to lock it before leaving?

Shit.

He hurried to the kitchen and checked the back door.

It was still locked, so she had not gone out that way.

The same had been true of the front door.

She was inside, somewhere.

He hurried to the cellar door, fear that she had fallen down the steps disappearing when he saw that the old child latch near the top was still engaged.

But where?

He headed over to the main stairway, disbelief that she would have gone up them dominating his mind.

But then where was she?

As unlikely as it would be for her to climb the steps, no other options were present. He had to go up and check.

MEL HEARD him walking back and forth, his steps heavy on the old farmhouse floors, her anxiety growing with each step.

What was he doing?

Why wasn't he coming up?

Easy.

She took a deep breath through her nose.

He would come up.

Of that, there was no doubt.

But when?

The question sparked the anxiety once again, and this time it was harder to push back down.

She took anther breath.

And another.

And another.

And another.

And then closed her eyes for a moment.

Count to—

A step groaned as weight settled upon it, the sound one that previously would have caused dread but now brought relief.

He was coming up.

Was she really ready for this?

How much more ready could she get?

Do or die.

JOSIAH HALTED, the sense that something was wrong having grown stronger with each step.

Gramma Matilda had come up here.

No evidence supported this yet, but he knew it to be true.

She had come up here and something horrible had happened.

Of this, there was no doubt.

Now he just had to know what it was that had unfolded.

And why.

The former would be easy to uncover, the latter...not so much.

Sometimes the why was never revealed.

He took a step, and then another, his body passing two doors that didn't interest him.

Whatever had happened, it had occurred in the room with the girl.

Once again, nothing but the simple fact that he knew this to be true guided his thoughts in this direction.

The door to her room was open.

He stepped in.

The girl was sitting on the bed, staring at him, eyes wide, body still secure.

She shifted her eyes to her right.

Josiah followed them.

Horror hit, his legs threatening to disappear.

A hand on the doorframe prevented his fall.

MEL HAD BEEN EXPECTING OUTRAGE, but instead all he gave was silence.

And tears.

They rolled down his cheeks, seeking routes through the crevasses where pieces of his face had been put back together.

Seeing this was a bit unnerving.

She didn't want him to express emotion.

She didn't want there to be a human side to him.

He wiped away the tears and turned toward Mel.

"What happened?" he asked.

Mel made a noise against the gag.

He nodded but made no move to free the gag, his attention turning back to the old woman.

Mel waited.

Seconds stretched into a minute and then two minutes, all while the man just stood there in the doorway, more tears falling.

Mel couldn't take it any longer.

She groaned against the gag.

He turned toward her once again, a questioning look on his face.

Mel groaned again and then motioned with her chin down toward her groin area, hoping he would think she had to pee.

He simply stared.

Mel sighed.

The man stepped into the room, halted, and then turned and left.

What? Mel thought, confusion replacing the anxiety. *No. Come back!*

She punctuated the thoughts with a scream against the gag, one that he likely did not hear as he headed down the steps.

Despair replaced the confusion.

He was going to leave her up there with the stiffening body.

He was—

Steps once again.

He was coming back up.

Hope returned and with it the anxiety.

The man came back into the room, and this time he did not hesitate in the doorway but went around to the side of the bed that did not have a dead body alongside it and took hold of the lock behind her head that held the gag in place.

. . .

"WHAT HAPPENED?" Josiah asked, voice trying to keep calm.

The girl took a moment to move her jaw around and then wiped the drool from her chin onto her shoulder.

"What happened?" he asked again, his own ears hearing impatience within his words.

"Please, I have to pee," she said.

"What happened?"

She cowered backward a bit, eyes gleaming with fear.

"I don't know," she said, voice rushed. "She came up here all of a sudden and started screaming about rats and was stomping her feet and hitting the walls and then she tripped over the chain and hit her head." She groaned. "Please, I can't hold it much longer. It has been—"

"Rats?" he muttered.

"Yes," the girl replied. "Please. I have to—"

He sighed and pulled out a key to release the padlock that was in the center of her chest, which freed her arms and would allow her body to slip out of the straitjacket.

A groan of relief arrived as she stretched her arms over her head, fingers wiggling and cracking, and then reached them behind herself to pop her back.

"Thank you so—" she started and then twisted.

He saw something coming toward him, something that he didn't register until it crashed into the side of his head, the blow creating a visible spark in his field of vision, one that had a pinprick of blackness in the center, blackness that began to expand.

"*Sergeant?*" a voice called.

"*Medic!*" another shouted. "*We need a medic.*"

Josiah grabbed at something, his hand recognizing a foot.

He heard a grunt.

"Sir, we have a medic coming."

Fingers tried to remove his hand from the ankle, but he refused to let it go, and then something struck him in the chest. A crack echoed as his ribs broke. Another blow forced the air from his lungs.

More voices and gunfire.

An explosion hit.

Someone leaned over him.

He swung a fist, catching the side of a face.

And then his fingers found a throat and squeezed.

The sounds of choking erupted, all while his fingers felt the struggles of the throat muscles in his grip.

Another blow landed, this one hitting a part of his shoulder that caused his entire arm to go numb.

He swung his other fist and felt it connect with something that let out a grunt.

Silence arrived.

He blinked several times, Kandahar fading while the bedroom came back into focus.

He turned his head, which was pulsating with pain, and saw the girl on her back, one hand on her head, the other holding something that he could not fully comprehend.

Pain flared as he tried to sit up, a hand quickly going to his chest to comfort the broken ribs.

It didn't help.

The girl moved a bit, a groan leaving her lips.

And then she sat up, her eyes momentarily dazed before focus returned to them. Hatred appeared. And rage.

She lunged, object raised.

Josiah scrambled backward, chest screaming, and then sprang up, the room spinning with the movement.

The girl missed him with the first swing and then tried with a second one, but her balance was not much better than his and she stumbled.

Josiah charged, his body slamming into hers and knocking her back into the wall, plaster cracking, his mind fighting to stay conscious amid the pain.

His hands found her throat.

Panic appeared in her eyes as he squeezed.

Excitement flowed as he pressed his body into hers, the pain momentarily fading.

She said something that he could not understand, all while her hands uselessly pounded against his arms.

He felt himself poking her, the sensation sending a shiver through him.

Another word tried to leave her mouth, one that may have been "*why?*"

An attempted knee to his groin followed, but his height was too high for her to reach the intended target, the knee simply hitting his inner thigh.

He grinned and then lifted her up in the air by her throat.

Her face turned red, veins bulging.

She kneed him again and this time was able to crush his ball sack, her body falling to the floor as his hands went down to cradle himself, the pain in his chest adding its own input into the situation.

She started to scramble away.

Gritting his teeth, he reached out and snagged her by the hair.

She screamed as he yanked her back, her body spinning around and slashing at him with her dirty fingernails, one breaking free as it got caught in the scar tissue of his forearm, another breaking halfway down.

He punched her, the blow catching her on the chin.

His second caught her shoulder.

After that, he grabbed her and threw her onto the bed, something—likely her ankle—cracking against wood as she landed.

Stunned, she didn't move, the only sign of life that of her chest rising and falling, and the blinking of her eyes.

He moved toward her, his hands ready to end this.

She shifted herself quickly and then sprang at him from the bed, a fist swinging his way.

It caught him in the side of the head, knocking all sense from him, the blow far heavier than it should have been.

And then her knee found his balls again.

He stumbled backward, body eventually finding the wall, his mind trying to regain control.

She dropped something before heading to the door, his eyes unable to register what it was, but his ears noting that *thunk* as it hit the floor.

"*No,*" he tried to shout as she stumbled through the doorway, body disappearing into the hallway.

He took a step to follow, but the room spun.

And then he was choking, blood having hit the back of his throat.

She was on the stairs.

Get up! his mind screamed.

He tried to obey, but just getting across the room was difficult, that punch she had delivered having knocked everything out of whack.

But how?

His eyes shifted to the object she had dropped.

A padlock.

The one from the chest that had secured all the straps of the straitjacket.

She had punched him while holding it.

Just the realization caused the room to spin.

He took a deep breath and then forced himself to move.

Downstairs he heard the front door open and then close.

Panic grew, his body stumbling into the hallway.

He nearly fell down the stairs and then tripped when trying to step over the deputy's body.

A few seconds later, he had the front door open, his eyes scanning the darkness.

The girl was nowhere to be seen.

PART TWO
THE ECLIPSE

SIX

BINOCULARS TO HIS EYES, Josiah watched as the Father was wheeled out into the courtyard by an orderly, a pair of those ridiculous eclipse glasses already on his face.

Relief arrived.

He hadn't known if the Father would be viewing the eclipse, the topic having never come up during their meetings. Now that it was clear he would be watching it, Josiah could focus on making contact with him, something which had not been possible in the days following the girl's escape.

He was a wanted man.

Local and state police were on the lookout for him, and though it wasn't mentioned in the news articles he had read, he was certain federal authorities were as well, both military and civilian.

Fortunately, they had no idea where to look.

They also were only showing photos of him from his early days in the military, so his scars were not on display. Why they would do that, he did not know, but he had scoured the web, seeking out every story he could find on the manhunt, and not a single one ever showed his post-incident face. Instead, they simply mentioned that he had suffered severe facial trauma while in Afghanistan.

Despite this, he knew he still had to be careful.

Especially around here.

People would recognize him. Even those who had never interacted with him would know who he was. His size and scars had made sure of that, though up until the recent news stories the conversations about him had likely carried a significant pity factor. Now that wouldn't be the case. Pity might still be present, but the implied horror of his actions would counter it to the point where they felt he needed serious help—help that the police and other law enforcement officials would provide.

They were wrong.

They all were the ones that needed help, help that he and the Father were trying to usher in.

But no one would see it that way.

Not yet.

Maybe not even during their lifetimes.

Maybe not ever.

Once the war between Heaven and Hell concluded, there would be things that had been noted and things that hadn't been. That was simply how the world worked. Every war had unsung heroes. Common soldiers who did their duty, day in and day out. Sometimes they were recognized, sometimes they weren't.

The incident.

He unknowingly touched the side of his face while thinking about this, a finger running along the channels where his flesh had been burned away and then grafted back together with skin from his inner thighs.

The military had praised him as a hero for his actions on

that day, only the actions they described were not what had unfolded.

Such was sometimes necessary for the greater good of a cause.

It was like sweeping up a dirty floor.

Once all the dust and debris was gone, the floor looked nice.

He blinked, his focus on the present situation returning, his right hand lifting the binoculars to his face once more.

Most of the residents of the compound were present.

This was good.

The more people who were out and about, the less likely it would be that his presence would be noted right away—if at all. Sure, there would be more sets of eyes that could see him, but given the eclipse itself, most of those eyes would be looking up—even those eyes that were supposed to be on the residents they cared for—and given the darkness that would set in and the eclipse glasses he would be wearing, chances were good that he could get in and out without a problem, the Father hopefully conveying instructions to him quickly to minimize the risk. He would simply be one of the many, which was better than one of the few.

Now he just had to time things correctly.

And make sure it wasn't a trap.

He had been watching the compound and the surrounding area since dawn and hadn't seen anything that seemed out of place. And really, he doubted the authorities would understand the significance of the compound beyond the fact that he had frequently pushed a mop down the hallways during the overnight hours.

Had that been why the Father hadn't wanted to see him the other day?

Had the Lord warned him that there would come a time

when he would be on the run, thereby making it so the authorities had no idea that he would need to make contact with the Father at some point to find out what his next course of action should be?

But if the Father had known things would come to this, why not warn him ahead of time?

Or were the specifics not known?

The Lord worked in mysterious ways.

Everyone knew that.

It was kind of like the military in that regard.

Ours is not to reason why...

He shook his head and turned his attention back to the courtyard, eyes focusing upon the Father and the orderly who no longer was standing next to him. Following that, he checked his watch. They still had a half hour before the total eclipse would take place. He would break cover about ten minutes before that and head toward the Father.

He put on the eclipse glasses so his eyes could get used to any distortion they presented while making his trek toward the Father.

Following that, he checked his sidearm, hand pulling it free and looking it over, even though he knew it was good to go.

The glasses had belonged to a kid named Brian, who was currently locked away with his family in a root cellar, and the gun to Deputy Blake, who he had simply left behind in his front hallway after the girl had fled.

He also had a rifle that was leaning against a tree, one that belonged to Brian's father.

He would leave that where it was while making contact with the Father, its only purpose today being one of holding people back should he have to flee, a few shots toward the compound making it unlikely that anyone would pursue him into the woods and beyond them to the house he was temporarily located in.

. . .

EVERYONE WAS LOOKING up as the sun disappeared behind the moon, Josiah going unnoticed as he made his way through the darkening courtyard toward the Father, his right hand ready to pull his sidearm if needed, his left pretending to shield his eyes while blocking his scars should anyone glance his way.

No one did.

As expected, they were all completely enthralled by the astrological display that God had provided, one that Josiah felt had been created simply so he could speak with the Father. The timing was too perfect to think otherwise. This was all part of the plan.

The Father was not looking up at the disappearing sun.

Instead, his head was resting on his chest, eclipse glasses ready to slide from his nose and fall from his face if he shifted.

No one was paying attention.

Josiah stepped up to him and then crouched down, a gentle "Father" leaving his lips.

The Father didn't react.

Josiah touched his hand and gave it a shake.

The Father stirred, the glasses falling from his face.

He had been sleeping.

Anger toward the staff appeared but then faded because without their incompetence, he would not have been able to get this close to the Father.

"Josiah?" the Father said, voice heavy with sleep.

"Yes, Father, it's me," he said. "It's Josiah."

"Fire of the Lord."

"Yes, Father. I'm here."

A withered hand took hold of his wrist, bony fingers digging in. "Wh-why?"

"Why what, Father?"

"Why?" the Father repeated.

Josiah didn't know how to reply because he didn't know what the Father was asking, so instead he asked, "What do I need to do, Father?"

"The child!" the Father gasped.

"What?" Josiah asked, head shifting to see if anyone had heard the Father.

No one seemed to notice.

"The child," the Father repeated.

"She got away," Josiah said.

The Father looked at him, confusion present.

"Josiah?" he asked.

"Yes, Father, it's me."

Drool appeared and ran down the Father's chin.

Anxiety began to build as Josiah used the small towel draped over the chair to wipe the drool away.

The Father smiled at him and then turned toward the disappearing sun, eyes looking straight at it without the glasses.

"A sign," the Father said. "Darkness."

Josiah smiled, the newfound clarity of the Father's voice what he had been waiting for. Hoping for.

"She is here."

The girl from the room? Josiah wondered, but didn't ask.

"Clothed in the sun," the Father continued, voice rising. "Protect her! From the Seven!"

This was familiar, the Father having once spoken something like this before. He would have to check his notebook. It was one of the few things he had taken from the house before fleeing with his bug-out bag.

"You must protect her!"

"Who?" Josiah asked.

"Protect her!"

"Who?" Josiah asked again. "Is it the girl from the room?"

"Clothed in the sun!"

"Father, please."

"Protect her from the Seven!"

"What girl?"

Without warning, the Father let out a shrill scream, a hand going up to his eyes.

"Father," Josiah said, hand going up to turn his face away from the sun.

"Hey," someone cried.

"His glasses," another shouted.

Josiah found the glasses and handed them to the orderly who knelt down on the opposite side of the Father, the young man's lips repeating the Father's name over and over again in a soothing voice that was trying to calm him.

Another joined the scene, saying something about getting him inside.

Josiah took a step back as they tried to push the wheel-chair, both forgetting that the brakes were set.

A hand touched his arm, a voice asking what happened.

Josiah turned and came face-to-face with Rhonda. She headed the Special Care department that the Father resided in. Her quizzical look turned to one of horror as she saw his scars and realized who he was.

"Security!" Rhonda shouted, voice somehow carrying over the commotion.

"It's him!" someone cried.

"Call the police!"

Josiah shot Rhonda in the leg and then turned the gun toward a security guard who was hurrying over, the bullet catching him in the upper chest.

Screams erupted.

Someone hit him in the back.

More gunshots echoed, though they were not from him.

Someone else had a gun.

An orderly several feet away from him fell to the ground, just as a resident in another wheelchair twitched as a bullet took out a chunk of his throat.

Josiah tried to see who was firing, but couldn't pinpoint them.

A bullet whizzed by his head.

He dropped into a crouch and looked around for the Father, his thinking being that maybe he should try to take him with him so that he could be there should the Father try to give more details on the girl he needed to protect.

Screams echoed, as did several more gunshots.

Orderlies, residents, and family members either fled the area or dropped to the ground, the only ones who didn't drop down being those who were in wheelchairs.

Josiah spotted the Father.

He was once again slumped in his chair about fifteen feet away from where Josiah crouched, the orderlies who had been trying to help wheel him back to the compound having obviously aborted their mission once the gunfire began.

Josiah hurried toward him, a decision to pick him up and carry him being made.

Blood oozed from the Father's mouth.

A bullet had caught him square in the chest.

Josiah couldn't believe it, his body going numb as he stared at the lifeless body.

Another gunshot echoed, this bullet hitting the chair and sending a ricochet up into his arm, the pain similar to a bee sting.

He shifted and looked toward where the gunshot had come from, his eyes seeing a young man taking aim. He was not an orderly, security guard, or resident, but appeared to simply be a family member.

Anger arrived.

Josiah charged the young man, who fired another wild shot in his direction, once again missing, his large body slamming into the kid before he could realign himself, gun leaving his fingers as his body crashed backward to the ground.

"You killed him!" Josiah screamed and then kicked the kid in the head, his boot feeling what he hoped to be the crunching of bone.

Several more kicks pulped the face, and then he leaned in and pressed the gun to his temple and fired.

Sirens echoed.

Josiah looked up and saw two county sheriff vehicles flying down the road.

They were still a good distance away.

He turned and headed toward the trees.

MEL DID NOT WATCH the eclipse.

She saw it and the darkness it created from her bedroom window, but she didn't go outside to experience it with everyone else in the neighborhood, lawn chairs, tables, and grills set up as if it were the Fourth of July rather than a simple Monday in August.

Well, simple probably wasn't the way to describe it.

Not when the astrological event taking place was a rarity.

Even so, it did not appeal to her.

A month earlier, it would have.

Now...*meh*.

And it wasn't alone.

Nothing really appealed to her.

Everything was *meh*.

Though she should have pretended some excitement because her mother was now making her see a shrink. A legit one with an office and everything instead of the hospital quack who had come to talk with her after her so-called "ordeal."

Ordeal.

That's what everyone called it.

It annoyed her, though she wasn't sure why.

Maybe because it felt as if all the adults had gotten together and quietly discussed how to refer to what had happened in a way that wouldn't cause trauma—like she was fragile and needed to be shielded, her mind and body ready to shatter if they used words like *kidnapped* or *abducted*.

She shook her head.

The appointment was at three.

She didn't want to go, but she didn't really have a choice.

Actually, she did have a choice, but enduring what would follow if she chose not to go wasn't how she wanted to spend the next several weeks, so she had given in. Plus, she didn't completely hate the idea of talking with someone. She didn't like it, and she didn't want to go at all, but a tiny part of her did think that being able to vent a bit might have a beneficial element. Even so, she wanted it to be on her terms, not her mother's. She also did not want her mother to be a part of it.

Hopefully, the shrink would agree with her.

One-on-one would be best.

If her mother needed to speak with someone about the *ordeal* and how it was impacting her life, she could find her own shrink to speak with, but doing a two-on-one thing with whoever it was she would be seeing at three would not work. Nope. Besides, she was pretty sure the only thing that was really affecting her mother was the fact that Mel was not playing the part of a rescued kidnapped victim that her mother had envisioned, one that would continue to bring her attention from the local news networks.

Teen Girl Escapes Psycho Serial Killer!

Goodbye local networks, hello national networks.

Interest was there. All Mel needed to do was say yes.

But she didn't.

And it was driving her mother crazy.

One big upside, things between her mother and boy toy Todd seemed to be unraveling.

Mel didn't know the exact reason for this, but she had a theory that her mother didn't want the age difference to become a talking point within the media.

It was almost enough to make Mel agree to the interview requests.

Almost being the key.

She sighed and looked at her new phone—her old one was locked away as evidence with the police, given that it had been at the scene of her father's murder.

Father's murder.

Her escape and the details she had provided the police had been a break they had desperately needed, though one that hadn't seemed to help them in locating the man named Joseph Ellis.

Joseph Ellis.

It felt weird having a name for the monster. It didn't feel right. And the pictures they frequently showed on the news and on the posters that had gone up were surreal because they did not match the face that she had stared at while fighting for her life.

No.

It was too clean.

Too perfect

Too "All-American Boy."

Plus, it didn't help answer the questions she had on why, though at least a connection between her father and the man had been established. They both worked for the old folks' home.

Had worked.

Beyond that, however, she was still lost.

Why had the man killed her father?

What reason could he possibly have had?

Nothing came to her.

The police seemed equally baffled.

As did the staff of the old folks' home.

One had been a part-time janitor, the other a doctor, and while it was possible the two had interacted with each other from time to time, it seemed unlikely that anything beyond simple workplace recognition would have developed.

Equally odd, both to her and the police, was why he had kept her in the room.

Though the detectives hadn't come right out and said it, they were confused as to his motive since she was adamant about not having been raped. At first, they had felt that maybe she had blocked it out, but her insistence on this and the tests they had run had forced everyone to admit that it had not happened.

Learning this had changed the entire focus of their investigation.

Initially, they had thought she was the reason her father had been killed, as if she had been stalked by some psycho serial killer who took her to his secret dungeon, her father having simply gotten in the way.

In reality, he had been the target, and she the afterthought.

It left everyone confused.

Her most of all.

And until that confusion was rectified, she could not move on. It was that simple. She had to understand what had happened. And why.

Until then, it would feel like she had an open wound that was festering beneath a bandage, one that would eventually get the better of her if she did not root out the infection.

Speaking of infection, she had antibiotics to take, which meant she also had to find some food.

THE FATHER WAS DEAD.

Josiah paced the first floor of the house while trying to come to terms with this, the adrenaline from the confrontation and shootout having faded considerably during his journey through the woods and across the river.

It was unthinkable.

Like Moses getting killed before freeing God's people from Egypt, or Paul falling off a cliff on the way to Damascus.

It just wasn't the way things were supposed to play out.

The Father was a tool of the Lord, and while tools of the Lord were often martyred, it wasn't until *after* they had fulfilled their part in God's plan.

Or were they?

What if God's successes throughout history with individuals such as Noah, Moses, David, Peter, and Paul were simply the tip of the iceberg when it came to His attempted use of individuals in the war between Heaven and Hell?

What if most fell before their purpose could be completed?

Would God allow for such a thing to happen?

Was it even a matter of Him allowing for things like that to happen?

Was that why there was a war?

Because while God was all-powerful, so was his adversary.

Did they counter each other out?

Careful...

Josiah shook the thoughts away and turned his focus onto what it was the Father had said before things had turned ugly.

"Clothed in the sun. Protect her from the Seven."

But who?

He needed a name.

Or a sign.

Something.

Just knowing there was a woman out there was not enough.

And if she was already being hunted, as the Father's words had implied, then that made things even worse because he was already a few steps behind the enemy.

He stopped pacing and went to the cupboard to get a glass so he could have some water, a realization that he was dehydrated arriving.

Following that, he grabbed a banana from the fruit bowl.

Healthy body, healthy mind.

He would need both.

Especially now.

With the Father gone, he could no longer wait to receive instructions on what he needed to do—not unless the Lord decided to provide them to him.

Nope.

Now he needed to look at the data, interpret it, and make the decisions.

Only he had no actual data.

All he knew was that there was someone out there who needed help.

And that it likely was not the girl who had escaped.

But then who?

No answers appeared.

And none would with him just standing in the kitchen thinking about it.

He needed to do something.

But what?

He ate the banana while thinking about this and then went and tried to turn on the TV, but once again the three clickers got the better of him, and rather than going down to retrieve the boy to help him, he simply stared at the dark screen while contemplating things.

. . .

"I THINK the biggest thing is that no one really believes me," Mel said, fingers fidgeting with a rubber ring toy that had been sitting in a small bowl next to the chair within the psychologist's office.

"Why do you say that?" Dr. Fletcher asked, his hands folded in his lap.

"I don't know. I just get a sense that everyone feels like I'm hiding something."

"Are you?"

Mel didn't reply.

Fletcher waited.

Mel sighed. "All he did was keep me in that room in a straitjacket chained to a bed."

"For two weeks."

"Yeah."

"Why?"

"How the fuck should I know?" Mel snapped.

Fletcher raised an eyebrow.

"Sorry," Mel muttered.

"For what?" Fletcher asked.

Mel stared for a moment and then just shook her head.

"I'm sure you can understand why some would find it odd," Fletcher said.

"I guess," Mel admitted. "Do you?"

"I find it curious."

"Curious?" she asked.

"A pretty teenage girl, kept chained up on a bed for two weeks. Most would assume the reason for that was so he could keep you as a sort of sex toy, yet he didn't touch you in that way. In fact, from what you've said, it seems like he tried to keep you clean and fed, and in as little discomfort as possible while still being secure."

Mel nodded.

"And he was caring for his grandmother."

"Who I killed," she muttered.

"Yet he didn't take it out on you. He only became violent after you struck him with the rolling pin."

Mel nodded.

"Why do you think that is?" he asked.

Mel shrugged.

"He was no stranger to violence and perfectly capable of killing. Yet the only time he displayed any violence toward you was when he was trying to subdue you, first in your father's place and then during your escape attempt."

Mel waited, but he didn't go on, so she asked, "What does it mean?"

"I have no idea," he said while lifting his hands. "And that's why it is so curious. Something is missing, something that prevents us from understanding what it was he was up to. Why did he kill your father? Why did he kidnap you? Was—"

Thunk! Thunk! Thunk!

Fletcher jumped at the sound and then turned toward the door as it opened, an angry statement leaving his lips as two familiar figures entered the office.

"Sorry, Doc," Detective Simmons said. "We need to speak with Mel."

Her mother was a few steps behind the detectives and quickly said, "Honey, that bad man shot up the old folks' home where—"

"This is outrageous," Fletcher voiced. "You can't just—"

"We have an active shooter situation," Simmons snapped.

"We are in the middle of a session!"

"This trumps that."

"Get out of here right now!"

"One more word and I'll have you arrested for interfering in an investigation."

"Arrested?" Fletcher laughed. "Good luck trying to explain that to the ACLU."

"Doc, if you prevent us from doing our job and put further lives at risk, I guarantee you and your staff will never be able to cross any street in this county without getting a ticket."

"Are you threatening me?" Fletcher asked, crossing his arms.

"You bet your Ivy League ass I am!" With that, Simmons stepped around Fletcher and took hold of Mel's arm.

"Don't you fucking touch me, you pig!" Mel snapped while yanking her shoulder away.

"Mel!" her mother gasped.

"Fuck you!" Mel shouted.

Her mother's face went white, disbelief spreading.

"Enough of this," Simmons said. "You're coming with us. If you don't like it, that's too bad."

Mel crossed her arms.

"She doesn't have to go with you if she doesn't want to," Fletcher said. "Not unless you have cause to detain her."

"People are dying!"

"Then go out there and stop him!" Mel shouted, throwing an arm toward the window. "I've answered all your questions a hundred times. I don't know anything!"

"He killed your father, and now he has killed the resident your father was assigned to at the facility where they both worked, as well as several others that were in the area watching the eclipse."

"What? Why?" Mel asked.

"That's what we want to figure out," Detective Higgins said, his soft voice finally entering into the fray. "And if you could help us in doing so, it would be greatly appreciated."

"But I don't know anything," Mel said, exhaustion arriving. "He never really talked to me all that much, and when he tried he was always really nervous."

"Nervous," Fletcher asked, intrigue present. "How so?"

Mel tossed her arms up into the air. "I don't know. Like first-dance nervous."

"First dance?"

"You know, when all the girls are on one side of the gym waiting for the boys on the other side to come over and talk to them. He was like one of those boys. Always seemed shy and unable to think of things to say to me, but wanted to say things. And he was always embarrassed about the food pouches."

"Food pouches?"

"Yeah, the kind that soldiers eat."

"MREs," Higgins said. "He bought them in bulk from an army surplus place in Conway."

"Ah," Fletcher said with a nod. He turned back to Mel. "And you say he was embarrassed about them?"

"Yeah."

"How so?"

"He would just apologize about them. Over and over again. All the time. And about not being able to cook. He would try sometimes, but I guess it never turned out well because he never brought up anything. It was weird. Annoying even. Almost like he wanted me to tell him it was okay."

"Did you?"

"Did I what?"

"Tell him the food pouches were okay?"

"Maybe a few times," she said with a shrug. "I don't know."

"And did that seem to help his nervousness?"

"Oh, for the love of God, this is not getting us any closer to figuring out where he went or what his next move might be," Simmons snapped.

"Getting into his head and trying to understand his thought process is the only way to figure out what his next move will be," Fletcher replied, voice stern.

"Really? Okay. Then tell me, based on the fact that he was

nervous when talking to girls, where would he have fled after shooting up the old folks' home?"

"Probably the same location that he has been in since fleeing his grandmother's home," Fletcher said.

"Which is...?"

Fletcher shrugged.

Simmons shook his head and turned to Higgins. "This is pointless. Let's go."

Higgins hesitated and then turned to Mel and said, "If you think of anything that might help, please let us know."

"Gee, and here I thought I would just keep it to myself," Mel replied.

Higgins stared at her for several seconds and then muttered something before turning toward the door.

"Detective," Fletcher called.

Higgins stopped and turned back. "Yeah?"

"Any idea where the straitjacket came from?"

"Straitjacket?"

"The one he kept Mel in during her two weeks of captivity."

"Oh...I'll have to check with forensics on that."

"Might want to make that your next stop because an honest-to-God professional-use straitjacket is not all that easy to come by."

Higgins thought about this for a second and nodded.

Mel's mother looked from Fletcher to the retreating detectives, a look of uncertainty on her face. And then she followed them out.

"Close the door, please," Fletcher called.

Mel grinned as the door was pulled shut.

Fletcher returned it.

"You really think the straitjacket is important?" she asked.

"Maybe," he said.

Mel waited, but he did not elaborate upon that.

. . .

JOSIAH HAD A BIBLE. It had been in his bug-out bag, along with two dozen MREs, maps, two extra pairs of clothes, ointment for his face, water purification tablets, a tin pot for boiling and cooking in, matches, a lighter, flint, toilet paper rolls stuffed with dryer lint and candlewax for starting fires, a knife, a hatchet, duct tape, and rope.

So far, the ointment, Bible, and three MREs were the only items he had pulled from the bag since leaving his grandmother's place, his previous stockpiling of goods up north at his fall-back position having provided everything he needed while waiting for the day of the eclipse to near.

And it would continue to provide once he returned within the next two days.

But then what?

The question had been bouncing around his mind all afternoon, ever since the shootout at the compound.

He had been anticipating instructions from the Father.

Something clear and precise, like when he had been ordered to go kill Joel, but instead he had gotten the vague statement about a girl being hunted by the Seven and his needing to find and protect her. It wasn't enough. Who was the girl? And the Seven?

It didn't make any sense to him.

He was a soldier, not a theologist.

Whatever meaning the statement had for the Father was lost on him.

And reading the Book of Revelation didn't seem to be helping.

The Father had been able to take the descriptions that were presented and point out what they were referencing within the modern world. Josiah could not. Even now, while flipping through the pages, he couldn't figure out who the Seven were or what the great eclipse had signaled.

And what about the seals that were being broken?

Which one were they on?

Josiah had asked the Father this question many times but never got any answers, the Father obviously feeling that such information was not needed for Josiah to complete his missions.

Josiah had always accepted this, but now wished he had pressed a bit more because such information could now be important.

Or was it?

The Lord had spoken through the Father, so if it were important for Josiah to know something, it would have been conveyed to him. And if it weren't important, it wouldn't be. In fact, maybe the lack of information on certain things was so that he could stay focused and not get distracted.

The girl.

He had to protect her from the Seven.

But who was she, and who were they?

Once again, his mind hit a wall.

Frustration billowed.

He didn't want to leave the house without an answer, without direction, without a mission.

He didn't want to head back to his fallback position just to wait, his days spent wandering the empty halls and the wilderness beyond without purpose.

He didn't want to—

Wander around the wilderness.

The thought was like a revelation, one that he couldn't believe he didn't recognize earlier.

Going out into the wilderness was exactly what he needed.

It was what all the great prophets had done, the isolation

and exposure helping to scrub free the mind so that God could enter into it.

The simplicity of it had made it almost impossible to see.

That was the problem with the modern world; it provided so many distractions—so many bells and whistles—that one often got all twisted up because they overcomplicated things.

He had fallen victim to it.

But that would soon change.

Once the sun set, he would start the journey back to the abandoned facility up north and then head off beyond it until he reached a spot where he could focus on clearing his mind of everything so that the Lord could speak to him and guide him toward his purpose.

It wouldn't happen right away.

The prophets always spent several weeks out in the deserts and mountains before their purposes were known to them, and the same would happen with him. But that was okay. He was trained to survive out in the wilderness and had done so in some of the harshest conditions nature could produce.

I was being prepared.

For this moment.

The Lord had known he would need these skills, not so he could camp out on the plains of Kandahar and in the mountains of Tora Bora, but so he could disappear following the eclipse and prepare himself for what would follow.

Instructions would be forthcoming once he was ready.

All he had to do was open himself up and the Lord would let him know who the girl was so that he could go protect her.

Or maybe just who the Seven were so he could eliminate them, thus protecting her without even ever having to interact with her, thereby allowing her to fulfill whatever purpose it was that she was destined for.

A new Mary?

One who would give birth to a child who would finally end the war between Heaven and Hell?

The Second Coming?

It was almost too much to even comprehend, yet somehow he knew this was what it was. Even he could see the signs. Mankind was coming to an end.

PART THREE
THE SEVEN

SEVEN

JOSEPH ELLIS.

The name began trending on Twitter within hours of the shooting at the old folks' home and was still going strong three days later. No one who was posting really knew all that much about him, but that didn't stop everyone from sharing their thoughts on him, guns, and the military.

People were also sharing their thoughts on her. It was surreal. And upsetting. People were cruel. She knew this before seeing her name on the list of trends, but she hadn't realized just how cruel they could be. Or how nasty. Every other status seemed to be talking about her body. Some even went so far as to claim she was being overly sensitive about the entire thing, considering that she had not been raped. And then there were those who felt she had staged her own abduction, Joseph Ellis being nothing more than a pawn in her scheme, one who had now snapped because she had made the police go after him as if he were a villain when really he was nothing more than a wounded warrior who had been forgotten by those who had sent him into battle.

Reading that one had left her speechless.

How could people actually believe such bullshit?

It was mind-boggling.

Facebook was no better.

Her inbox was full of messages. Some were sympathetic, but most were from guys talking about what they would have done with her had she been their captive.

It was sick.

One person had even sent photos of himself masturbating upon various pictures of her, statements on how he knew she would just love having his hot spunk spurting all over her face.

Prior to her "ordeal," she had used the block button maybe five times in six years. Now, barely a day went by when she wasn't blocking at least five people, if not more.

Not that it made much of a difference.

Creating a profile was not that difficult. One person who she had blocked had actually created a new one and sent her an angry post about being blocked within ten minutes of her having blocked him.

And then there was the poop guy.

One night he had pummeled her with questions asking how she had used the bathroom while locked up, her phone alerting her to all his messages upon waking up the next morning.

Did you have any accidents?

Did he make you wear a diaper?

Did he give you enemas?

Did he like it if you pooped yourself?

Did he poop on you?

Did you poop on him?

Anger had eventually developed, her lack of replies to his questions somehow an attack against him and those who shared his interests.

Blocked!

And then there was all the talk about Father Preston.

Up until the shooting, Mel had never really known much about what it was her father did at the old folks' home, but apparently one of his jobs had been to care for an eighty-three-year-old pervert who had been suffering from dementia and was in the end stages of his life, an end stage that no family member would visit him during, given the history he had with them and the cult-like church he had created after the Vietnam War.

Why her father had never mentioned the man was beyond her, but she had a feeling there were probably confidentiality rules with the old folks' home that he hadn't wanted to break. Also, why would he want to talk about it? The stuff people were sharing about the man was horrifying, especially since he had never gone to jail for any of it. People even stood up for him, many of them being the parents who had willingly brought children to him, children who he had defiled in the name of God.

Pull over! I want off this planet!

"THERE'S no question about it, Father Preston was batshit crazy," Fletcher said.

Mel blinked.

"Not what you were expecting me to say?" he asked.

"It was less clinical sounding than I had anticipated."

He grinned.

"I read that he castrated himself," Mel said.

"I read that as well, though I haven't been able to confirm it."

"Is that common with cult leaders?"

"Unfortunately, no. Taking teenage brides and having sex with children is the more prevalent behavior when it comes to cult leaders, especially the Christian-themed ones."

"And the parents allow it," she noted, disgust present.

He nodded.

"Why?"

"It's difficult to fully grasp the mindset of someone that has been taken in by a cult. Religion itself is about making rational people believe irrational things, but most are able to segment it into their lives in such a way that it doesn't impact their ability to function on a day-to-day basis. With a cult, this is not the case. It comes to dominate one's life. Every aspect of it. All or nothing. In a sense, it is the most pure form of religious practice. Primal even. Nothing but the religion matters. Choice is gone. A person becomes a slave to their deity, which means they are really a slave to the 'chosen' messenger of the deity. Father Preston, David Koresh, Jim Jones...all became 'God' to their followers since their voice was the voice of God. They can do no wrong. And to question them would be akin to questioning God."

"I just don't get it," Mel said. "How could a person let themselves become like that?"

Fletcher held up his hands and said, "I wish I knew."

Nothing followed for several seconds.

"This information on Father Preston," Fletcher prompted. "Did you just stumble upon it, or have you been actively looking into him and trying to find information on him?"

"Mmm, both I guess," Mel said. "At first it was because his name was trending, but then I started Googling him because of the connection with my father. After that, I learned about the Children of Light and started reading about that. One thing led to another."

Fletcher nodded. "Like going down the rabbit hole."

"What?"

"Lewis Carroll. *Alice in Wonderland.*"

Mel just stared at him.

"Eh, doesn't matter," Fletcher said with a wave of his hand.

"Any particular reason you have been looking into all this stuff?"

Mel shrugged. "I'm trying to find answers."

"Answers for?"

"Why my father was killed," she said. "There has to be a reason. It wasn't random. He didn't just decide to kill my father one day. Something prompted it. I want to know what."

"So do the police."

"No, not really."

"Why do you say that?"

"They're only interested in catching him, not understanding why. All their questions are aimed toward figuring out where he is."

"But once they catch him they will be able to interview him and find out why he has done the things he's done."

"No. Whatever comes out after that won't be real. Not once lawyers get involved and they all try to work out the best way to bring this thing to a close."

"Hmm."

Mel waited, fingers fidgeting with a new rubber gadget that had been in the fidget bowl.

"Do you have any theories? Ones that you were trying to maybe prove with your research. Or at least point toward."

"Sort of," she said. "But it didn't really pan out."

"What was it?"

She shook her head. "Doesn't really matter."

"Melinda."

She looked at him, the use of her name a sign that she needed to elaborate.

He waited.

She let out a breath. "I wanted to find out if he had been molested by Father Preston as a kid and then planned on killing him, but then my father found out, so he killed him first so that he wouldn't warn anyone." She made a dismissive wave. "It was dumb."

"I don't think so," Fletcher said.

"It was. The two were not connected at all. He isn't even the right age. And if my father had learned something about him planning on killing Father Preston, why wouldn't he have warned someone right away? It's not like he was killed at work. He was at home."

"The theory still has weight. It's just the details that might need some tweaking."

"What do you mean?"

"Maybe your father did overhear something, but it wasn't as extreme as 'I'm going to kill Father Preston.' In fact, from what it sounds like, Father Preston may have been caught in a crossfire, which means that Joseph Ellis's intent might not have been for him to be killed at all."

Mel nodded.

Initially praised as a hero, many were now calling into question the idea that the late Edward Goodman had prevented further bloodshed by pulling out a gun and opening fire on Joseph Ellis. Nothing official had come out since the investigation was still ongoing, but witness statements and a quote from an anonymous person within the investigation seemed to be giving the theory momentum. This had led some on the right to claim that the witnesses were crisis actors who had been hired by the left to try to discredit gun owners and chip away at the Second Amendment. It didn't take much research to disprove this, but that didn't seem to stop the claims.

"But if he didn't go there to kill Father Preston, what was he doing there?" Mel asked.

"That's the million-dollar question," Fletcher said.

. . .

GETTING to his fallback position was easier than he had anticipated, likely due to the maps the kid had helped him pull up and print out on the computer after the shooting. Without those, he would not have been able to reach the safety of the compound. The police would have caught him in their net. But reach it he did.

The Father would have been proud.

Sadness followed.

His death had obviously been the will of the Lord, yet even so it hurt.

Such deaths always did.

Seeing the old chapel within the facility added to his emotion.

He had been hoping to bring the Father here once it was ready, the secret renovations something he had been engaged in for several months.

Now that would never happen.

But that was okay.

His mind had envisioned a future where the Father would hold services in the refurnished chapel, his words helping to prepare his flock for the end that was coming, but such was not to be. The Lord had different plans, plans that were far more important than the work he had been doing within the old structure.

Now he just had to await instructions so he could take part in those plans.

Heading out into the wilderness beyond the old abandoned facility would be the first step. After that, the Lord would guide him toward the second one and then the third. Of this he had no doubt.

HIS SUPPLIES!

They were scattered all about, the boxes he had carefully

stacked in a corner and hidden with debris from the crumbling structure having been opened and rummaged through at some point during the last few days.

Rats?

No.

The MREs had been ripped open, not chewed, some of the contents dumped about rather than eaten. And someone had built a fire. Right in the middle of the old commons room. They had used pieces of rotted wood from some of the collapsed parts of the compound. Most of it had not burned, the singed remains still in the pile that had blackened the concrete floor.

He touched the wood.

It was cool.

The fire had died out several hours earlier.

But that didn't mean whoever had built it was gone.

And even if they were gone, they might return.

He had to do a search.

Room by room.

This was his sanctuary, one that he had spent quite a bit of time stockpiling supplies in. And now someone had disturbed it. All his hard work ruined.

Anger warmed his blood.

He pulled the pistol from his waistband, thumb flipping the safety off, and then took a deep breath.

THE COMPOUND WAS large and somewhat difficult to progress through systematically due to areas that had collapsed during its long period of abandonment. Fortunately, Josiah had reconned it enough times during his early days to know how to maneuver from one room to the next without incident. He also knew all the choke points that would make for a good defense should an assault be made upon it, as well as several escape routes to get into the woods beyond. And then there were the secret areas that could be accessed through the basement levels. He didn't know the original purpose for those areas, though he feared it might have been for experimentation. What exactly such experimentation would have yielded he did not know, but many of the rooms had been so well hidden that they had remained untouched until his discovery of them.

Memories of the comics he had read as a kid appeared, memories that made him wonder if any superheroes or supervillains had been created.

If so, could that have been who had gone through and destroyed his supplies?

Had someone returned seeking answers?

Fear that such a person would be evil and working against him arrived. Science was Satan's domain, his most powerful tool in pulling humanity away from God.

Could that be why he was there now?

Did the Lord want him to confront whatever it was that had returned?

He would have to wait and see.

One thing was clear.

Unless they were really good at hiding, whoever or whatever it was that had ruined his supplies was not there.

EIGHT

"MELINDA?" a voice called.

Startled, Mel twisted, eyes searching for the speaker while her right hand slipped into her coat pocket and secured a small bottle of pepper spray.

A young man was standing by the wall, just beyond the Forever 21 display window, a Cardinals hat pulled low, hands in his coat pockets, one foot bent backward, the sole of his boot pressed against the faux brick.

"Not interested," she said and turned to walk away.

"You sure?" he asked.

She did not reply, her feet taking her away from the young man, who did not follow, his body staying against the wall as she continued down the corridor.

"MEDIUM CHAI TEA LATTE," Mel said to the pink-haired girl behind the counter. "Extra sugar."

"You know, you just asked for a tea tea latte," a voice said.

Mel spun.

The young man was standing behind her, a grin on his face.

"What the fuck?" Mel demanded, hand quickly going into her coat pocket. "Are you following me?"

"What?" he asked. "No! I just thought I'd grab a cup of tea while shopping, and what do you know, here you are. Great minds and all that."

"Leave me alone," she snapped.

"That'll be five sixty-eight," the pink-haired girl said.

"I got this," the young man announced, pulling out a wad of cash. "And add a second one to the order."

"Extra sugar?"

"Always," he said.

The pink-haired girl totaled up everything and then made change from his twenty, all while a second girl, this one with natural-colored hair, put together the drinks.

Once the drinks were ready, Mel snatched hers and started to walk away.

"Whoa, whoa, hold up," the young man said. "I just want to talk."

"Yeah, well I don't," Mel said.

"Even if it's about Joe?"

Mel twisted back and eyed him for a moment. "You a reporter?"

"No," he said with a laugh.

"Then why do you want to talk about...*him*?" She still didn't like voicing his name.

"Because he saved my life in Kandahar."

Mel blinked. "Kandahar?"

"It's in Afghanistan."

"I know where it is," she snapped, the statement a lie.

"Sorry," he said.

"So...you're a soldier?"

"I was," he said with a nod and then motioned toward a table. "Ten minutes."

Mel looked around, unsure.

"After that, you'll never see me again," he added.

"IT WAS JUST SUPPOSED to be a meet and greet—a hearts and minds type of thing where we introduced ourselves to a village elder and his family in hopes of creating a bond that would eventually lead them to help us identify members of the Taliban and any other jihadists that were in the area," Nelson said and then took a sip of tea.

Nothing else followed.

"I take it things didn't go according to plan," Mel said after several seconds, and then took her own sip of tea.

"No, they certainly did not," he said, his eyes looking at her but obviously not seeing her.

Mel waited.

"They hit Joe first. I'm not sure what exactly happened, but I know he was lured into a back room in the elder's house, which was quite a bit larger than the typical houses within the village, but still something we would consider primitive by our standards." He shook his head. "Everything was pretty chill at that point. They served us tea and a goat. Not all of us were sitting down to eat since security was our first priority, but we all did get a glass of the tea and hunks of meat folded in flatbread. I remember it was while I was standing by a short wall, keeping an eye out on the fields and a drainage area when I heard the scream. It came from within the elder's house. I was the first one in, and it was bad."

Something crashed nearby, causing Mel to jump.

Nelson simply stared, that faraway look still in his eyes.

And then he sipped some more of his tea.

"It's hard to say exactly what happened, but from all the

bits and pieces it seems that Joe discovered some sort of weapons stockpile while in the back room, which was when the elder's daughter hit him in the side of the head with a lantern that shattered and spewed burning kerosene all over him. I got in while he was flopping around on the floor trying to put himself out. It was bad. I actually saw a chunk of his face peel away as if it were the crispy skin on a freshly roasted chicken. Slid right off and fell to the dirt floor."

Mel paused with her tea halfway to her lips.

Nelson saw this and uttered an apology.

"What happened to the daughter?" Mel asked, voice barely audible.

"I killed her."

Mel blinked.

"She had a weapon when I entered the room, one that she had been about to use to finish off Joe. I took her out before she could." He sighed. "I regret it to this day."

"Killing her?"

"Getting in there before she finished the job."

Mel stared at him.

"Pain. It's the only word that can be used to describe Joe's existence following the attack. In any other era, his wounds would have killed him, but now our medical technology has gotten to the point where it can keep someone in his condition alive, but can't keep them from being in pain. At least not without the aid of painkillers, which can only be used for so long, and even with them, those first several months were pure agony. Burns and skin grafts are the worst. I have never experienced it myself, but I know several who have. It's horrible. One actually has to break in the grafted flesh so that it doesn't lock up and make movement impossible as it heals." He sighed. "Can you imagine that? Having to fight against the scar tissue so it doesn't tighten too much and make movement impossible."

"No," Mel whispered.

"Me either." Another pause. "It fucked up his mind. All those meds, all that pain, and a government that tries but fails miserably when dealing with the psychological health of those that come back." Another sip. "It was only a matter of time before something like this happened."

"Something like what?" she asked.

"Sorry?"

"He killed my father, kept me in a straitjacket for two weeks, and then went to an old folks' retirement home with a gun, which led to a shootout where several people were killed," she said. "Is that the 'something like this' that was inevitable?"

He shrugged.

She mirrored the shrug.

He stared at her.

"Why did you seek me out?" she asked. "Was it just to share a sob story about what he went through so that I might feel sorry for him?"

He didn't reply.

"Because if so, fuck that. It sucks what happened, but that doesn't change anything. My dad is still dead. Those people at the old folks' home are still dead. And I'm still...shit, I don't even know what I am at this point."

He held up a hand and said, "I wasn't trying to justify what he did or make what you went through any less horrific. I just thought you might be interested to know what happened to him."

"Well, I'm not," she snapped.

"I get that. And I apologize."

"Anything else?" she asked, arms crossed.

"Just one question and then I'll leave you alone."

She sighed.

"Where do you think he went?"

"Oh, for fucks sake," she said and stood up.

"Whoa, whoa," he said, standing up himself. "Wait!"

"Why does everyone think I know where he went?" she demanded, voice raised to the point where others turned to see what was unfolding.

Nelson looked around and said, "Sorry. Stupid question. How about this instead? Do you really believe he went south to join up with that militia group, because I think that's total bullshit?"

This caught her off guard. "Why?"

"It was all too obvious. He put the police on a false trail, one that they fell for hook, line, and sinker."

"Fuck," she said.

"It was pretty genius really, especially now that the group is being uncooperative."

He was right. The group was the focus now. Had been the moment the kid had pointed the police to the computer that he had helped *him* use. They even questioned her on if he had ever said anything about being a member of the militia group, at which point she had once again reiterated the fact that he never spoke to her about anything beyond the food he served her.

And the kid was now a hero. That was the most annoying thing of all. Everyone acted as if it was remarkable that an eleven-year-old would think to point the police toward a computer that the man had used. How was that remarkable? Tons of eleven-year-olds would have done the same. Kids were not as simple-minded as adults liked to believe.

"And now the question is," he continued. "Did he do this because he was planning on staying in this area or because he just wanted to be able to escape what he knew would be a pretty significant law-enforcement net?"

She didn't reply to that.

"And if he is still in the area, will he try to get you back?"

"I wasn't the reason he killed my father," she said, exhaustion arriving given that she seemed to have to explain this to everyone.

"Not initially, but he kept you for two weeks, which means something about you triggered something within him that made it so you were important to whatever it was he was doing. If this hadn't been the case, he would have eliminated you. Same with the kid and his family. He kept them alive. Why? So they would point the police in the wrong direction once he fled. But with you..." He simply held up his hands.

"Why would I be important to him?" she asked, wary.

"That I don't know," he said with a shake of the head.

"Well, if you find out, be sure to let me know."

"Whoa, wait a second," he said as she started to walk away.

"You said one question and then you'd leave me alone."

"Yeah, but that was before we established that he likely will be coming after you."

"He's not going to come after me."

"You don't know that."

She shook her head.

"I can help you."

"I don't need any help."

"You sure about that?"

"I did okay the first time around."

"You were held captive for two weeks and only escaped because he slipped up. Sorry if I don't see that as a resounding victory."

"Whatever," she said and waved a hand at him.

"Come on," he said.

She started to walk away, but then stopped and turned back.

A glimmer of hope appeared in his eyes.

"How do I know you're not helping him?" she asked.

"What?"

"An old army buddy, one who probably is just as fucked

up from everything he saw over there as he is, who just happens to show up after all the shit hits the fan. Sounds a bit convenient."

"Convenient?"

She nodded.

"I don't even know how to reply to that."

"Then I guess we're done."

"I guess so."

She waited a few seconds and then once again started to walk away.

This time, he did not follow.

NINE

TWO DAYS CAME and went without any signs of the intruders, which led Josiah to wonder if their presence within the old compound had been a one-time thing.

A one-time thing where they destroyed my supplies and tried to build a fire?

Why?

The question went unanswered.

They always did when alone.

He ate an MRE while thinking about this.

Not all of them had been ruined, just most of them. And the ones that were left seemed to consist of his least favorite entrees. Not that one could really claim a favorite from the pouches, but one could certainly have least favorites. He had learned this early on during his military career. He had also learned that his opinion on the meal wasn't important. All that mattered was getting the nutrition it provided.

And then what?

This was another question that didn't seem to have any answer.

Simply put, he didn't know.

A week ago, before he had arrived at the compound, he had planned on heading out in the wilderness and waiting for the Lord to give him a sign, but after finding the evidence of the intruders, that no longer seemed like the correct path.

So he waited.

And waited.

And waited.

Nothing.

Heading out in the wilderness like a prophet of old didn't seem right, but neither did sitting around twiddling his thumbs waiting.

Something had to happen.

Soon.

He was Josiah.

He had a purpose.

The Father had made this very clear early on.

Only the purpose was not being fulfilled.

Be patient, an inner voice soothed.

The Lord had guided him to the Father and would guide him again.

He just had to have faith.

He just—

Voices!

Somewhere out beyond the compound.

He couldn't make out the words that were being spoken, but it was clear that someone was out there. And not just one someone, but at least two, maybe more.

THREE INTRUDERS.

Two men and a woman.

They entered the compound through the west side, which was the same side he had entered through upon his discovery of this place last year.

Such was to be expected.

Portions of the west side had collapsed, likely from storms, which made entering the compound fairly easy. Once inside, things became more difficult. Rot had ruined many of the walls and floors, which had led to internal collapses, some of which had blocked off hallways and stairways. In some areas, plants had even started to grow from seeds that had gotten inside, which was somewhat surreal.

Josiah knew how to navigate through it all, thanks to several systematic walk-throughs.

The intruders did not.

They got lost several times and had to backtrack through the hallways to junctions they had chosen poorly on, their voices oblivious to his presence given how vocal they were. These voices also revealed that they had been there before, an angry shout of, "I thought you said you remembered the way!" echoing from one of the males, which sparked a shouted reply and then what sounded like someone being slammed into a wall, all while the young woman alternated between laughing and telling them to stop.

Were they the ones who had damaged his supplies?

He would soon have an answer to that. And to other questions, ones that they would answer.

First though, he had to wait for the right moment to hit them.

Three to one were not bad odds for him, not with his size and skill, but it still paid to do things right, which meant waiting for them to arrive at one of the choke points. Once they did that, he would take out whoever was in the rear, which would spur the other two deeper into the compound, at which point he wouldn't have to worry about them getting back to the collapsed area and fleeing into the fields.

They were getting closer.

He waited, his hands ready for the strike.

He was not going to use the gun, not unless it became absolutely necessary.

The reasons for this were simple. He had a limited supply of ammo, and he wanted them alive.

"Can't interrogate a dead person!"

The words were those of a CIA operative who had been pissed with their squad for not bringing back any prisoners after a raid on a mud hut.

Prisoners had not been their objective.

They never were.

And if the operative had wanted someone to take back to the Salt Pit, he should have used Delta. Or some PMCs.

Josiah's team was a search-and-destroy team.

It was that simple.

They killed the enemy.

That was it.

At least it had been in the beginning.

Eventually things did change.

Whether it was for the better or worse remained to be seen. Most of his team thought it was the latter. He, however, had no opinion. He had just done what was instructed. Up until that day...

Blue eyes.

Soft skin.

Tears.

Screams.

Fire!

He could still feel it eating away his flesh, his own screams echoing throughout his mind.

They would never go away.

Sometimes they dulled, but never to the point where they weren't there, a constant reminder of what would happen if he were cast down into the lake of fire, his soul damned.

An eternity of being burned.

He could not let that happen.

Not for him, and not for others.

Satan had to be destroyed.

Once and for all.

He could not fail.

"Oh shit!" a voice snapped, dragging him back to the present.

He blinked.

The three were staring at him.

He had wandered from his ambush position and stood in the middle of the hallway.

They ran, or at least they tried to, the two males crashing into each other as they spun, one tripping over the other.

The girl was a bit more nimble and started down the hallway, the sounds of her shoes echoing upon the old linoleum surfaces as she tried to retrace her steps toward an exit.

He had to get her.

If he didn't, it would only be a matter of time before the police realized he was not down south with a militia group.

Once that happened...

No. It couldn't happen.

This was his fallback position, his Alamo.

There was nowhere else to go.

He had to stop her.

First, the men.

They were easy to disable.

All he had to do was break their knees.

He got the first one, who was still on the ground, the fall having jarred him. A simple blow with his booted heel did the trick, the snap echoing, followed by a horrible scream.

The other took more effort, his body having managed to get up and start to run, but not with enough distance to get away, Josiah giving him a shove from behind that forced him through a rotting wall.

After that, breaking his knee was easy.

Quiet too, this one going into shock after the blow without even letting out a scream.

The girl.

She had taken a left up ahead at a T junction, one that led to an old stairwell, bathrooms, and a cafeteria. A few offices in an administrative area were that way as well, but one couldn't get to them from the hallway due to debris and instead had to go up to the second floor and then drop down through the ceiling.

She wouldn't be doing that.

Even if she headed into the stairwell rather than heading toward the cafeteria and administrative area.

It didn't go up, only down.

And if she went down, she would be stuck, though she wouldn't know it at first. In fact, it would look promising upon her first glimpse of the level as she stepped off the stairs, given that it opened up to a long hallway that stretched nearly a third of the length of the compound itself. Problem was, she would be below ground, and in an area that was designed to prevent escape should any of the unstable patients get out of their rooms.

SHE ATTACKED him in the stairwell, which caught him off guard, her hands wielding a chunk of wood that she had picked up at some point before hiding behind some boxes beneath the stairway.

Unfortunately for her, the wood was rotted and snapped as it slammed into his arm, which he had instinctively raised to block the blow he had sensed at the last second, the girl having aimed for his ear.

Eyes wide, she backed up until she was against the wall, nothing but a foot of splintered wood now in her hands.

Josiah stared at her.

She was shaking, though whether it was from fear or something else was beyond his ability to know, the scabs, sores, and bruises that were upon her face and bare arms making him think there was more going on within her body than a simple fading of adrenaline.

She was a junkie.

And the two men upstairs?

Were they junkies too?

"Put it down," he said.

She growled at him. Literally. Growled.

"I'm not going to hurt you," he added.

She lunged, his right arm easily deflecting the splintered piece of wood while his left hit her in the side of the head. It wasn't much of a blow, but it was enough to stun her, his arms easily scooping up her frail frame and putting her over a shoulder.

Following that, he carried her up the stairs, her body staying still until he reached the main level, at which point she seemed to go into an angry feline mode and started scratching at him with her nails and trying to hit him with her knees.

"Stop!" he shouted, throwing her to the ground.

She scrambled back and then tried to get to her feet but wasn't quick enough, his right hand getting a chunk of her hair and pulling.

Screams echoed as he dragged her by the hair, all while her hands clawed at his grip.

It was no use.

His scar tissue on that hand was tougher than her nails, several of them breaking free as they tried to tear chunks from his hardened flesh.

HE PUT the two men into an old janitorial closet, the laces

from their shoes connecting their broken knees together so that if either moved it would cause unbearable pain. He also tied their wrists behind their backs. It was probably overkill, but since the door to the closet was missing a knob, he didn't want to leave anything to chance.

The girl he brought to the main room, her hands cuffed behind her back, her thin delicate wrists almost too small for the metal links to be effective.

She sat in the corner, twitching.

He watched her.

Track marks lined her arms, which made him think heroin, though he wasn't positive. Drugs weren't something he had much experience with, unless one counted all the different pills and painkillers he had been on after the *incident,* but he knew enough to know that heroin wasn't the only thing that could be injected.

Her shaking grew worse and worse.

"P-p-please, n-n-need a f-f-fix," she eventually begged.

"Of what?" he asked.

She wouldn't say, though he didn't think it was because she was being stubborn. Instead, she simply couldn't answer, the shaking growing too intense.

"Meth?" he asked.

She didn't reply, just kept twitching.

He waited, thinking maybe the twitching would stop.

It didn't.

She mumbled something that he didn't understand.

For a moment he considered asking her to repeat herself, but then realized she wasn't trying to talk to him. She was simply speaking gibberish while going through withdrawal.

"HELP ME."

Josiah opened his eyes and looked over at the girl.

She was staring at him from the corner, her cuffed hands now in front of her, fingers clasped together in her lap, her body bathed in light from the setting sun that streamed in through one of the windows near the top of the commons room wall.

A chill slithered through him.

Not only had he drifted off to sleep while leaning against the wall, but he had done so while the girl was untethered, her body free to move around if she so desired. And with her hands now in front, she could have easily grabbed the gun and shot him.

It was a huge slip-up, yet one the girl had not taken advantage of.

Why?

Something felt different.

He could sense it in the air.

It was as if something else were in the room.

Something powerful.

And it was protecting him.

Shielding him.

From her?

Was that why she hadn't gone for the gun while he slept?

Had some unseen presence prevented it?

Rather than wait for an answer, which he knew would not arrive, he pushed himself up from the wall and asked, "You hungry?"

The girl didn't reply.

"Thirsty?" he pressed.

Nothing.

"You sure?"

Still nothing, her eyes simply glaring at him from where she sat in the square of light.

Sunlight!

Clothed in the sun!

Is this what the Father had meant?

Is she the one?

His mind pondered this as he went to retrieve some water for himself.

Did the Lord guide the three to the compound so that I would find her?

The question lingered within his mind as he uncapped a water bottle and downed nearly half of the liquid within.

No answer arrived.

But that was okay.

As long as the Lord kept guiding everyone into their proper position so things went according to His plan, all would be well. He didn't need to question or speculate, just wait for the gentle unseen push.

And there had been quite a few unseen pushes, ones that he wouldn't have realized were pushes if he hadn't known he was a tool of the Lord.

Was that why I tried to help the elder's daughter?

Had he not done that, and then gotten burned, he never would have ended up living with his grandmother and working at the old folks' home. And if he had never ended up working there, he wouldn't have ended up getting turned around during his first week on the job and found himself in the Father's room. And if he hadn't found himself in the Father's room, he never would—

Something buzzed.

He spun, eyes back on the girl, who now had a look of panic on her face.

Another buzz.

Something was in her hands.

Understanding arrived.

No!

Dropping the bottle, he raced toward the girl, his left hand catching a foot as she tried to kick him, his other grabbing at her hands, which squirmed every which way before he was able to get at what she held.

Cell phone.

Seeing it simply confirmed his fear, his hand nearly throwing the thing on the ground to destroy it before he thought better of it and instead looked at the screen.

Missed call.

Billy.

"Who's Billy?" he demanded.

She glared.

"Who is he?" he snapped.

She grinned.

"Who!"

"You're dead," she hissed and then let out a phlegmy cackle.

He turned his attention back toward the phone, his fingers fumbling with the screen, trying to see if there was any way to gather more information on who this Billy was.

"What's the password?"

She simply laughed.

He kicked her, right in the ankle.

She shouted with pain, and then went on laughing.

He squeezed the phone, fingers pressing into the screen, which began to give, and then loosened his grip.

Deep breath.

And a second.

And a third.

"They're gonna kill you when they get here," she continued, her laughter fading.

He didn't reply, just glared.

"And then we're gonna cook tons of shit in the basement and make serious scratch, all while you're rotting in the field."

He grabbed her throat, fingers squeezing, the muscles

within pulsating, his penis growing as blood vessels within her eyes started to pop. "How many?" he demanded.

She couldn't answer, not with his fingers squeezing her throat.

"Four?" he asked.

She clawed and kicked.

"Five? Six?"

More clawing.

And then her bladder released.

"Seven?"

She nodded.

The Seven!

His fingers opened, releasing her throat, a horrible gagging sound echoing as she tried to suck in air within the dusty sunlight.

She really is the one.

The Lord had brought her to him.

And he had almost killed her.

The thought made his legs go weak.

He stumbled over to the wall and leaned against it until he had control.

The girl was on the ground, still struggling, her cuffed wrists creating a small buffer between her chin and the floor as she sucked in air.

Seven were coming.

Seven that knew he was here and were ready for him.

And not just any seven, but the Seven.

This could get tricky.

And the girl would be no help.

How do you protect someone who wants you dead?

This wasn't the first time he had asked this question, it being a common one while in Afghanistan, yet now it somehow felt more prudent than ever before.

He had to protect her.

Not just for her sake, but all of humanity.

The burden was his.

I'm ready.

At least he was mentally.

Physically, he had to prepare.

It would take some time for the Seven to arrive.

How much, he didn't exactly know, but he had a feeling it would be enough to get things in order so that he could take care of them as they tried to locate her.

First things first, he had to secure her.

And he knew the perfect spot for it.

She wouldn't like it, but then she wouldn't like a lot of things in the next several days. But it was for her own good. Given her state of being, he not only had to protect her from the Seven, but from herself as well.

TEN

MEL COULDN'T STOP THINKING about her encounter with Nelson. It had seemed so random yet was anything but. He had sought her out and then followed her to the mall, all while she had been completely oblivious to his presence. It was unacceptable. Had he actually been out to harm her, she would now either be dead or a captive once again.

Could he really be working with *him*?

Say his name.

No.

Coward.

Joseph Ellis!

Joe!

She didn't like it.

She didn't want him to seem normal—to seem human—and with a name like Joe, it was difficult not to picture the face the media kept displaying when talking about him.

"*But he is human,*" Fletcher had said. "*We all are.*"

Mel had simply rolled her eyes at that.

"*Facing his name and his humanity is the first step toward moving on,*" Fletcher had added.

"*I don't want to move on.*"

"*Why?*"

"*Because he's still out there.*"

Still out there.

Waiting...

Watching...

For me?

She wanted to laugh away the idea but couldn't. Not after what Nelson had implied. She might not have been *his* original focus, but once she entered into the scene, she had become one of the pieces. An important piece it now seemed.

But why?

As always, no answers followed.

She couldn't even begin to speculate upon it, given how out of the norm those two weeks had been.

Actually, that wasn't true. She knew it had something to do with her father and the old folks' home. Beyond that though, it was nothing but a parade of question marks.

THOUGH HER FATHER had worked there for several years, Mel had never actually visited the old folks' home. It just wasn't something one did, not unless they had a relative living within, and even then such visits were usually considered chores by the younger members of the family.

Now she sat outside the building, getting her first glimpse of the structure that had been prominent on the news for several days, their angles quite different from the one she now had from the visitor lot since they had been kept back near the main road. Some stations had also used footage from overhead, though they had been careful about what they had shown since the public frowned upon seeing actual bodies lying about.

This is dumb, she told herself and then got out of the car, her left foot instantly twisting on the heels she had chosen to wear.

"DO YOU HAVE AN APPOINTMENT?" the receptionist asked.

"No, but it is important that I see whoever it is that would be in charge of the ward that Father Preston was in," Mel said.

"I'm sorry, but requests for interviews have to go through our public relations department."

"I'm not a reporter," Mel said.

"Oh."

"My father worked here. Father Preston was one of the residents he cared for."

"I see, and what is your father's name?"

Mel gave it to the lady, who didn't seem to recognize it at all.

"Okay, I do see your father in our directory, though it looks like he is unavailable right now."

"That's because he was murdered."

Eyes wide, the receptionist slowly turned to look at her.

And then it clicked. "Oh my God, your father was...and you are..."

"Yes, and I would like to speak with someone who can answer some questions for me on what exactly it was my father was doing and why it led to him being murdered."

"I don't know if—"

"Or I could just start talking to reporters, who are all very curious about this place, though I would hate to give them a false idea of what goes on here, especially considering all the negative press right now."

"Let me see if I can get Ms. Hayden to come down," the receptionist said. "If you want to have a seat, I'm sure it will only be a few moments."

"Thank you," Mel said and carefully walked over to the little waiting area that had been set up, her mind once again cursing the idea of wearing heels. The skirt, blouse, and jacket had also probably been a bit much.

"MELINDA, MY DEAR," Ms. Hayden said as if they knew each other. "I'm so sorry about what happened to your father. Let me be the first to say that everyone here is thinking about him and the horrible events that have unfolded these past several weeks."

Mel blinked.

Talk about overplaying things. She even put a hand against her own chest, almost as if she had to reassure herself that her heart was still beating.

"Um...thanks," Mel said.

"Is there anything we can do? As you can imagine, we are still a bit overwhelmed by everything that has happened, but even so, that won't stop us from trying to help the families of our team members who lost loved ones in this heartbreaking tragedy."

Oh brother.

"Actually, there is. As you are probably aware, I accidentally walked into my father's house while he was being...while Joseph Ellis was killing him."

"Horrible. Just horrible."

"Yeah," Mel agreed. "Anyway, I'd like to know more about my father's role here and why Joseph Ellis would have fixated on him."

"My dear, I can't possibly understand the motivations of that *former* employee."

Mel held up a hand. "I'm not asking you to get inside his head. I just want to know how they would have known each other. That way I can try to understand how this all happened and start to put it behind me."

"They were coworkers."

"They were *not* coworkers. My father was a doctor that specialized in dementia while Joseph Ellis mopped the hallway floors and dumped out trash bins. How would they have gotten to know each other?"

"Well, my dear, you know how your father was. Very friendly and always accommodating to those who were suffering, and Joseph Ellis was obviously suffering. Everyone could see that. So I'm sure your father befriended him and—"

"Cut the bullshit."

Ms. Hayden's jaw about hit the desk.

"One worked during the day while the other worked part time at night. They weren't even orbiting the same sphere of existence."

Ms. Hayden just stared at her.

"How did the two know each other? And how was Father Preston involved?"

"My dear, I know you're upset, but I don't think that calls for speaking to me this way and—"

"I'm sorry, you're right," Mel said. "Coming here was a bad idea."

Ms. Hayden gave a sympathetic nod. "It's understandable. With everything you've been through. Just remember that we all—"

"Speaking with reporters would be better," Mel said, cutting her off. "They're just as curious as me, and they know all the different angles one can use to get at the truth of the matter."

"Truth? What truth? We're not hiding anything here."

"I'm sure they'll be able to get to the bottom of that," Mel said, standing, hands smoothing down her skirt before she headed to the door. It was a stall tactic, one that she hoped would work because she was totally bluffing. She wasn't going to go to any reporters. This pretty much was her last grasp at trying to figure things out.

"Wait, wait, let's just go over everything one more time, just so we know we aren't leaving any stones unturned."

"Ohhhhkayyy," Mel said, returning to her seat.

Several seconds came and went.

"What stones have we failed to overturn?" Mel asked.

"There was an incident"—she held up a hand, stopping herself—"not an incident. A situation. Something your father was involved in."

"With Joseph Ellis?" Mel asked, heart starting to beat faster.

"Yes. And Father Preston."

Mel waited.

Nothing else followed.

"What was it?" Mel asked.

"You do understand, this is off the record," Ms. Hayden said.

"What record? I just want to know why Joseph Ellis fixated on my father and then kidnapped me for two weeks."

"I don't even know if this played a part in that," Ms. Hayden said. "And even if it did, there is no way we could have predicted such an extreme reaction."

"What happened?" Mel asked, voice insistent.

"It was kind of heartbreaking, actually. During his first week here on the job, Joseph Ellis had a bit of a panic attack and found himself lost and unable to figure out where to go, which led him into Father Preston's room. We're not sure why, but his presence triggered something within Father Preston that brought a bit of clarity to his mind. The two were discovered sitting side by side in Father Preston's room talking. *Talking*. An actual conversation. Your father was blown away by this when he found out and encouraged Joseph to sit in with Father Preston on a regular basis. It was completely unorthodox, but since it seemed to be getting results, we went along with it."

Mel waited, but when nothing followed asked, "And?"

"That's it."

"What do you mean that's it?"

"That's how your father and Joseph knew each other. They actually got quite close too. I'm surprised your father never mentioned him."

"How close?"

"Beers after work. Dinners together at the local diner. Like I said, your father was a very friendly person. And a bit lonely. The two bonded."

"So why did he kill him?"

Ms. Hayden shook her head and said, "I really can't say."

"Did something happen? Did they have a falling-out?"

"I don't know."

"I think you do."

Ms. Hayden held up her hands, the gesture one of hope- lessness.

"How long did these talks go on for?" Mel asked.

"Quite some time," Ms. Hayden said. "Nearly a year."

"A year?"

Ms. Hayden nodded.

"And were they documented?"

"I do believe your father kept notes."

"Can I see them?"

"We don't have them."

"Why not?"

"They were your father's."

"And what, he didn't keep anything here? Records. Some- thing official. Progress reports."

"Like I said, this was a highly unorthodox thing that was taking place."

"So unorthodox that you don't want word of it getting out, given what has happened."

Ms. Hayden did not respond to that.

"I want to see those notes."

"I don't have them."

"Then who does?"

"Like I said, they were your father's notes, so I assume he would have had them."

Mel shook her head. "If he had had them, then the police would have them, and if the police had them, I would not have had to come all the way out here to find out how my father and Joseph knew each other."

Ms. Hayden shrugged.

Mel mimicked the shrug and then said, "I know you have them."

"Why would I have them?" Ms. Hayden asked.

"To protect yourself."

"To protect myself?"

"Obviously."

"My dear, I think you're starting to reach for things that are a bit far-fetched. Now, if you'll excuse me, I do have a meeting that I need to attend to." She stood.

"I'll find those notes," Mel said.

"I hope you do and that they provide some closure for you." She motioned toward the door.

Mel stood and turned, her steps careful so that she did not wobble on the stupid heels as she left the office.

She's hiding something, an inner voice said. *Has to be.*

Maybe not, another voice countered.

Maybe Ms. Hayden was right and Mel simply had been reaching.

But then why not mention the "unorthodox meetings" from the start? Could something like that really hurt the facility? Or was it just her career she was worried about? Would it even have an impact? After all, her father had been the expert, so if he felt such meetings might help, then who was she to say no? Could she even say no?

Mel didn't know enough about the protocols within an assisted living facility to answer these questions. One thing she did know: Ms. Hayden was concerned, so if need be, she could play that to her advantage. She also now knew that her father had notes. She didn't know where they were or how she would find them, but she knew they existed. How could they not? A breakthrough with a patient suffering from dementia would be huge. Even a minor one could lead to great things. And lord knows, he had needed something like that, something that would help motivate him upward and onward.

ELEVEN

SECONDS TURNED TO MINUTES, which stretched into hours that then doubled up upon themselves, all without the Seven showing up. But that was okay. They would come, and when they did, he would be ready.

Questions on who they might be bounced around within his mind, the speculation helping to keep him focused.

The girl had said something about cooking.

Meth?

It seemed likely given the area, though he couldn't say for sure given his ignorance of the drug trade.

One thing he did know: the girl and her two companions had been users, and whatever it was they had been using had really messed them up.

Would the same be true of the Seven?

The girl had made it seem like they were all partners since she used the term "we" when talking about all of them using this place to cook, but that might simply have been a drug-induced misconception, one that the Seven used to their advantage to keep her close and hooked on their product. In reality, the Seven could be clean, middle-class business people who sold drugs as side income. Teachers, police officers, bankers...anyone could be led astray when money was involved.

NO ONE CAME.

He waited until long after the sun had set, his body perched up on the roof of the building, eyes focused upon the old road that led to the old crumbling parking lot, his plan being to get a good look at the Seven so that he could assess how best to ambush them once they entered the compound.

Instead, he had simply been chewed up by mosquitoes, the nasty little bloodsuckers having swarmed in as the sun started to set and focused upon the unscarred areas of his flesh.

Frustration arrived.

Why didn't they come?

Had the girl been mistaken about how important she was to them?

Had her call for help fallen upon deaf ears?

If so, why had he been tasked with protecting her?

It didn't seem she needed it, not if they were able to let her go so easily.

Unless his keeping her here so that she couldn't go back to them was the protection she needed.

No.

That couldn't be it.

It was too simple.

He was a warrior, not a babysitter, one who had been specifically chosen by God because of the skills he possessed.

And the Seven were likely specifically chosen by the other side...

This thought silenced all the others that had been floating around within his mind. It also sent a chill slithering through his system, one that seemed immune to the August heat that was lingering into the night.

Here he had been sitting on the roof, waiting, without really knowing anything about the enemy beyond how many there were, his mind completely forgetting the fact that God wasn't the only one who could pick and choose warriors to use in this war.

It was a mistake that could have been costly.

One never wanted to underestimate the enemy.

History was rife with examples of what could happen when such mistakes were made.

This could have been the last time.

The fate of humanity was at stake.

He couldn't make any mistakes.

If he did...

He pulled out his lighter and thumbed a flame into existence while searching for an area of unmarked flesh.

You know what you have to do, the Father said.

No!

Yes.

Please no!

You have to commit yourself fully.

I can't!

Nothing else followed.

Josiah dropped to his knees, the lighter falling from his fingers, the flame vanishing.

He didn't want to do it.

He couldn't do it.

But if he didn't...

Tears began to fall from his eyes.

You have to do it.

This time the voice was his own rather than the Father's.

He had put it off for far too long.

It was now or never, and if he chose never, then it would doom everyone.

A little pain now was better than an eternity of pain.

A little pain?

No.

This would be more than just a little.

And that was why he had hesitated for so long.

It was so extreme.

Not just in terms of pain, but finalization.

Burning off tattoos or his nipples was one thing, but this...

It was too much!

But that was why it needed to be done, to prove his devotion.

God had chosen him, but had he chosen God?

He said he did, but actions always spoke louder than words.

He had known this his entire life, though it wasn't until he had met the Father that he realized how important the idiom would be.

Why me?

Why was I chosen?

"It is not for us to reason why," he said, voice sounding off as it broke the silence that had descended upon the dark roof.

Jesus had doubts too.

He wasn't sure if the voice was his own, the Father's, or the Lord's.

No, not the Lord's. He would have said "I," not "Jesus," for he was Jesus.

Can the Father really communicate with me?

In his mind, he pictured the Father standing before him like Obi-Wan or some other dead Jedi warrior that needed to communicate with Luke from beyond.

He wished real life were like that.

It would make things easier.

But then one's faith would not be as meaningful.

One needed doubt in order to have faith.

Without it, it just didn't have a purpose.

That was the beauty of—

A sound!

Somewhere out beyond the old parking area.

He pushed himself up from his knees and scrambled over to the edge, eyes blinking several times to clear the tears.

No one was down there.

At least no one he could see.

The Seven?

Had they been waiting this entire time?

If so, it added credibility to his recent thoughts on how they had been chosen for their skills and would be a formidable foe.

One might be making noise now while the others infiltrated the far end of the compound.

No! No! No!

He hurried across the roof and through the door that he had propped open earlier so that it would not make a sound when the Seven arrived, his feet taking him down three flights of stairs until he was on the main level, and then down a hallway that he saw more in his mind than for real, given how dark the corridors were now that night had fallen.

Nothing seemed amiss as he neared what he considered the main room, but even so he crept up on it, his senses on full alert.

It was empty.

From there, he checked on the two men who had arrived with the girl, both having been positioned on opposite sides of the compound so as to sow confusion with their screams and pleas once the Seven arrived.

One screamed at him to be let down, the pain of being

forced to stand on his broken ankle obviously too much for him. The other just stared, chest streaked with vomit.

He left both as they were and went to check on the girl, his hands forced to switch on a flashlight as he made the descent into the subterranean regions of the compound. It was simply too dark and the areas too complex for him to go at it by memory alone.

The girl was still secure, her tiny wrists locked to an overhead pipe that protruded from the wall within an old storage room that was still stocked with various items from when the facility was in operation. It was a cruel position, one that he planned on making more comfortable for her by bringing in some boxes for her to sit on, but for now she would have to stay standing.

THE COMPOUND HAD NOT BEEN INFILTRATED.

It took nearly three hours to determine this, his body methodically searching each room after his descent into the subterranean corridors to check on the girl.

Following that, he headed back down to see if he could speak with her and learn about the Seven, his thinking being that if he knew where they were located, he could hit them before they hit him, thus eliminating the threat to the girl and fulfilling his mission.

She did not want to talk to him, a statement of "fuck you!" making this pretty clear after he entered the small room.

"I'm not here to hurt you," Josiah said, voice soft.

"Then let me down," she snapped, wrist rattling the cuffs against the pipe.

"Tell me about the Seven."

"The what?"

"The Seven."

She simply stared at him.

"If you tell me about the Seven, I'll let you down," he said.

"What do you want to know?" she asked.

"Everything."

"Everything," she voiced.

He nodded and then waited, but nothing followed.

"Who's Billy?" he prompted.

"Billy?" she asked.

"You called him and then he called you," he said, pulling out her phone and giving it a jiggle.

"Oh, *that* Billy."

"Who is he?"

"Just some dumb tweaker that I used to fuck for glass."

Josiah blinked.

She grinned. "Jealous?"

He mumbled something that his own ears couldn't even decipher.

"You totally want to fuck me, don't you?" she said, body leaning toward him as far as the handcuffs would allow.

"N-no," he stammered.

She stared at him, somewhat puzzled.

"The Seven," he said, shifting things back. "Who are they?"

"How the fuck should I know?" she asked, body sagging a bit.

"You said they were coming."

"When?"

"After you made the call!"

"Whatever. I say a lot of shit when I'm buzzing."

"Buzzing?"

"Tweaking."

He shook his head.

"Jonesing for a hit."

"Meth?" he asked.

Her eyes brightened. "You have some?"

"What? No!"

"But you cook, right?"

"No."

The brightness faded, her body sagging against the bonds. "Billy would have some," she said, voice barely audible.

Josiah didn't know how to reply to that.

"You said he called?" she asked.

"Yes," he confirmed.

"Then maybe he has some," she said, hope returning. "You could call him. Let him know I'm here and I'll suck him off for a hit."

"Suck him off?" Josiah questioned, horror rising.

"I'll suck you off too for making the call," she said. "Please. I need it. Bad."

Josiah took a step back.

"No! No! Please! I give good head."

He took another step back.

"Or you can fuck me. Cunt, ass, I don't care. Just call him!"

He grabbed the flashlight, the sudden shift causing the shadows to dance along the walls.

"Please!" she cried, tears exploding.

He stepped out of the room, his right hand closing the door against her sobs, the growing stiffness in his pants hard to ignore.

HE SAT against the door to the storage room for fifteen minutes, his mind barely able to function.

How could she be the chosen one?

A drug-addicted nymphomaniac?

It didn't make any sense.

Why would the Lord choose—

Mary Magdalene.

It was like a lightbulb going off in his mind, one that pushed away all the shadows of doubt that were creeping in.

She had been one of the first to walk with Jesus.

A whore who eventually became a saint.

And now another had been chosen.

It was like everything was coming full circle.

Poetic.

But also troubling.

Not in a sense that the Lord should have chosen differently, but in the fact that this was going to be really difficult.

Or was it?

Could he use her addiction to get information on the Seven?

Was Billy part of the Seven?

A drug pusher would fit the mold for the type of person who would be working for Satan, though would he really be part of the Seven?

Only one way to find out.

He went back into the storage closet, phone in hand.

The girl looked up at him, hope present.

"You really want me to call Billy?" he asked, hand showing her the phone.

"Y-yes!" she stammered, head nodding.

"Does he know about this place and how to get here?"

"Yes."

"How?"

"Everyone knows about this place," she said, a puzzled look on her face.

"Everyone?" he asked, startled.

"Duh! Please! Call him!"

"Okay, okay, what's your password?"

"Password?"

"On your phone."

She groaned and let her body collapse within the restraints.

"I can't call him without your password," he said.

"Eleven thirty," she said.

"Eleven thirty?"

"Yes! Come on! Call him!"

"Okay, okay."

He thumbed in the digits and watched as the phone unlocked, a background picture of a young woman with a baby and a young man appearing behind a display of icons.

A few seconds later, he held the phone up to his ear as if making a call.

"No! No! No!" she cried when he lowered the phone with a shake of his head. "Try again."

"It's late. Maybe he's sleeping."

"He'll get up!" she shouted.

"I'll wait until morning."

"Please! Call him now!"

Josiah shook his head.

"Please!"

"Okay, one more time, but if he doesn't answer, I'm going to bed."

She waited, lips pressed tight, the look in her eyes a mixture of hope and terror.

He waited about twenty seconds and then lowered the phone.

"No!" she wailed, body collapsing to the point where she simply hung from her wrists.

"I'm sorry," Josiah said. "We'll try again in the morning."

She didn't reply.

He left the cell, door once again closing against her sobs, a sense of accomplishment present within his mind.

Her phone was now unlocked.

He had access to everything and everyone that was important to her.

It might not lead him to the Seven right away, but it was a good start. Things were moving in the right direction. The hopelessness he had felt a week earlier was fading. He was on the path that he was meant to be on, one that the Lord had chosen for him. Now all he had to do was follow it.

You still have to purify yourself.

The voice dulled the sense of accomplishment he had been feeling.

He didn't want to do it.

Not yet.

Not ever.

But he had to.

If he didn't...

"*You will fail,*" the Father had warned.

He remembered the flames eating away at his flesh, his mind unable to think of anything but the pain.

It had lasted less than a minute—he had been told—yet had felt like an eternity, which it would eventually be if he failed.

And not just for you.

All of mankind.

TWELVE

MEL SAT outside her father's house, eyes watching a strand of old crime scene tape flutter in the gentle night breeze.

Would it really be in there?

No.

The police would have taken it.

Or would they?

Of course they would.

But maybe not.

The debate had raged within her mind for hours—ever since leaving the old folks' home—until she couldn't take it any longer and decided to simply go to her father's house and have a look.

Now, however, she hesitated, memories of what had happened playing across her mind's eye.

And not just memories.

No one had witnessed her father's murder, but enough evidence had been gathered for the police to put together a solid theory on what had unfolded in the time before her arrival. Finding his chopped-up body in the landfill had helped them in this regard, as did the bits of blood and flesh that had gotten caught in the drain of the bathtub that sat in the bathroom of her father's bedroom.

Chopped up.

And put into garbage bags.

Mel shook her head in an attempt to rid herself of the imagery, but all she managed to do was shift over to the sight of the man standing naked in the bedroom.

Scars.

At the time she had seen them but didn't really focus on them, given the onset of terror. Now she did, the statements from Nelson having removed an element of mystery to the disfigurement.

Sympathy tried to slither in.

She halted it.

What happened to him had been horrible. Of that, there was no question. But horrible things had happened to many of the soldiers who were sent overseas, and they didn't come back and chop people up so that they could be tossed out in the next day's trash.

Why didn't he kill me?

Everything always circled back to this. It didn't matter how far out her thoughts had gone, eventually it all landed back upon this question, which then drifted into the "why did he kill my father?" territory.

Nothing had prevented her murder.

If he had wanted to, he could have killed her and then disposed of her.

But he hadn't.

Why?

What was she missing?

Whatever piece it was, she felt like it was within her reach, especially now that she knew her father and...*he*...had been acquainted.

That had been the key.

Now she just had to find the lock it fit into.

It won't be in there.

But maybe it will.

The police would have found it.

Do the police even know to look for it?

This thought led to one that questioned whether the police knew about the "unorthodox" sessions that had been taking place at the old folks' home. If not, then there was a chance that they didn't really know to focus on that as part of the motive for his murder. And now, given that they knew who the murderer was, they might not even really be investigating the "why" all that much. Not when their focus was on capture.

It was what the public wanted.

Plus, evidence was gathered for two reasons: first, to figure out who was responsible for the crime; second, to help weight the deck in favor of the prosecution during the trial.

As things stood, the police knew who was responsible, and when...*if*...it went to trial the prosecution would have no trouble convincing a jury to issue a guilty verdict. Not after what had happened at the old folks' home. It would be a slam dunk.

This meant it was up to her.

If she wanted to know the why of things, she had to figure it out for herself.

HOLY SHIT!

It was the only thing her mind could think to express as the smell of the house greeted her.

Nothing had been cleaned.

The kitchen, which had already been unbearable during her last visit, had been allowed to sit for weeks in the August heat, and while the AC had still been running—thankfully—

there was only so much it could do to halt the growth that had occurred upon all the food that had been left to rot.

They just left it, was her next thought.

This led to a question on if that was normal.

It was something she had never thought about before.

Once the police were finished with a crime scene, who cleaned it?

Was it left up to the family?

What if it was bloody?

Did the family really have to endure the horror of that, scrubbing away at a mess that would be a constant reminder of the tragedy they had experienced?

Or was this different?

The kitchen wasn't part of the crime itself, so maybe it wasn't something they would address after the fact.

Who will?

Is it even safe to be in the kitchen at this point?

The house itself?

Fear crept into her thoughts, and for a moment she considered aborting this stupid plan.

But then she decided against that, her thinking being that as long as she stayed out of the kitchen she should be okay.

Before doing that, though, she needed a way to keep the smell at bay.

Or at least muffled a bit.

Her bedroom held what she hoped would be the key, her shirt pulled to cover her nose and mouth as she hurried by the door to the kitchen and down the hallway to the bedroom.

THE POLICE HAD GONE through her things.

Why she had not anticipated this was beyond her, yet she hadn't, and now she felt completely violated by it. Humiliated too. Her room at her father's house was where she had kept things that she didn't want her mother to see. She didn't want her father to see them either, but he didn't snoop the way her mother did, so keeping things here had always been the best option when a locker at school was not available.

Focus!

Candle.

Matches.

Once the two were secured, she left the bedroom and headed to her father's study, the candle held a few inches beneath her nose, the apple cinnamon scent helping to keep the worst of the stink at bay.

NOTHING.

She spent nearly an hour going through her father's things within the study, and not a single item within the mess connected to the meetings that had been taking place at the old folks' home.

It was frustrating.

I might never know the reason why.

No.

She didn't want to accept that possibility.

Couldn't accept it.

Answers were available.

She just needed to find them.

Maybe it was time to talk to the police?

The thought brought about a sigh.

She didn't want to engage with them but felt like she might not have a choice.

If they had collected her father's things, then it probably meant the answers were sitting in their evidence room, collecting dust.

No.

If they had had information connecting everything

together like that, they would have located her in that bedroom while locked up in the straitjacket. There was no way around that. The police would have interviewed those who were connected with her father, especially those who he had had a falling out with, and that would have led them right to her.

If there were notes on those sessions, which she knew there were, then someone had them, someone who had not turned them over to the police.

Someone who might be trying to protect herself and her career.

Or did *he* have them?

Could that have been a part of the reason why he had killed her father?

Had something come out during the sessions that *he* wanted kept secret?

If that were the case, then she would never find his notes. Not unless she found *him* before the police did, and that was not a quest she wanted to put herself through. Once was bad enough. A second time...nope.

THIRTEEN

JOSIAH DIDN'T SLEEP.

He had wanted to, had planned to, but didn't, an innocent glance into the girl's phone having quickly turned into a perverted perusing of her photos, videos, and text exchanges.

She truly was a whore.

And not just in person.

Her phone had icons on it for various webcam sites, ones that she could log into with a few clicks and start broadcasting from, the phone camera capturing everything.

It was crazy.

Startling too, especially since he almost started broadcasting by mistake when exploring the icons.

Low battery.

The message popped up as he was staring at a photo of her wearing nothing but red panties, her arms positioned in such a way as to thrust her exposed breasts toward the camera, the pink nipples standing tall, all while she gave a wicked smile.

It was his favorite so far, one that seemed to hypnotize him, the low battery message the only thing that could tear him away.

And tear him away it did.

Panic arrived.

He couldn't believe it.

Here he had sat down to try to find potential info on the Seven, and all he had managed to do was piss away the entire night scrolling through her photos and watching video clips, his hand occasionally rubbing himself through his pants. It was pathetic. He was pathetic.

Josiah was supposed to be better than this.

He was supposed to better than this.

And now the phone was almost dead, all because he had let himself get sidelined by earthly temptations.

A sigh left his lips as his tired body slowly stood up, joints popping with relief.

The low battery message disappeared with a tap of his thumb, the picture of the whore once again displayed before him without any obstructions.

What would it be like?

Hand gently caressing her breast, palm ever so lightly touching the tip of the nipple...

His erection returned, pre-fluids oozing.

Would touching be okay?

Just to see what it felt like?

No!

The inner voice was so loud that he knew it could not have originated within his own mind, yet even so he argued against it.

Nothing else followed.

Startled, he voiced an apology.

Nothing.

He repeated the apology.

Still nothing.

No! No! No! his mind cried, body dropping down to his knees.

Seconds turned to minutes, his mind silently begging forgiveness, his lips joining in when those first pleas didn't get any response.

How long this went on, he did not know, but eventually he realized it was accomplishing nothing and that his actions would prove what needed to be proved.

If you had purified yourself fully, this wouldn't even be an issue.

This inner voice was his own.

Rather than reply, he let the words fade into his mind while standing back up, his joints once again expressing relief.

A yawn followed.

He rode it out and then gave his own cheek a brisk slap since sleep would have to wait. His stupidity in running out the battery on the phone had made sure of this. He needed to find a way to charge it, which meant he needed to find a phone charger. And a place with electricity so that he could plug it in.

The car.

One of the guys had been carrying a set of keys in his pocket, keys that he had set aside during his panicked preparations following the girl's call for help and his fear that the Seven were descending upon the compound.

And then they had slipped from his mind.

Why?

Such was not like him.

An abandoned car near the abandoned compound could attract attention, which was something he didn't want.

He was slipping.

Because of her?

His mind shifted back to the photo on her phone.

Stop!

The photo disappeared from his thoughts, but then was replaced by a video she had taken, one where she was on her knees, the guy holding the phone for her so that her actions could be viewed over and over again by anyone who held the device.

Had she sent it to people?

Was it used as a sort of ad to show what she would do for drugs?

The question lingered in his mind as he went for the keys, his body passing by one of the men he had trussed up to a post, the smell of piss and shit reaching his nose.

Keys in hand, he walked up to the man.

Terror appeared within the weary eyes.

"You three drove here," Josiah said.

The man muttered something that he couldn't make out.

Josiah waited.

Another mutter, one that might have been a request for water.

"Where's the car?" Josiah asked.

Another mumble, this one definitely a request for water.

"Tell me where the car is."

"Fuck you."

Josiah stepped behind the man, took hold of his right index finger, and broke it.

The scream echoed for several seconds.

"Where's the car?"

"Not far," the man whimpered.

Josiah squeezed the broken finger.

"Please!" the man cried.

"Where is it?" Josiah demanded.

"On the road leading in."

"How far?"

"By the gate!"

"On the road or pulled off?" Josiah asked, voice firm as he tightened his grip on the finger.

"W-what?" the man asked, the word turning into an unintelligible cry.

"Is it hidden or visible?"

"I-I-I don't know."

Josiah considered breaking another finger but then realized it would be pointless. Instead, he would simply go to the car and see for himself where it was located.

HESITATION ARRIVED as he started to leave the compound, a question of whether he should go down and check on the girl entering into his thoughts. Desire was behind the question. He knew this from the start. One fueled by the pictures and videos. Yet even so, he didn't dismiss it right away. A purified person would have. But he was not yet purified.

"If you don't do it, you will fail..."

THE CAR WAS NOT HIDDEN at all. It stood like a beacon in the middle of the road, parked just a few feet from the padlocked gate, a beacon that he should have snubbed out right after the three had been subdued.

It was only by the grace of God that it had gone unnoticed.

I'm protected.

But for how much longer?

He shook the question away while slipping through the gate, its presence across the road more of a suggestion against trespassing than an actual deterrent, given that one could simply push against the bottom corner to create an opening big enough to squeeze through.

A moment later he was peering through the grimy window on the passenger side, eyes trying to get a feel for things before he opened one of the doors.

Nothing within seemed amiss...unless one counted all the garbage.

The three liked fast food.

McDonald's and Taco Bell seemed to be the two favorites. Sonic came in third.

Steeling himself against the wretched smell that would likely emerge, Josiah opened the passenger-side door and quickly hurried around to open the driver-side door, his breath held the entire time until he could get a good fifteen feet away.

One minute came and went, and then a second and a third before he began his exploration of the interior.

The smell was bad, but not overbearing.

He had experienced worse.

Joel's kitchen.

Just the thought made him shudder, his mind still unable to comprehend how anyone could live like that. And a doctor no less. He should have known better. But then, he had been through a lot. The two had talked about it quite a bit while drinking after work, Josiah always having a simple Coke or root beer while Joel tried to drown himself with booze to the point where Josiah had to take him home.

To say the man had been a wreck would have been an understatement.

His life had fallen apart.

All because of his wife.

She too had been a whore, one who had infected his mind and body to the point where he couldn't rid himself of her.

It was sad.

Frustrating too because nothing Josiah could say or do seemed to help.

It reminded him of the woes he had often heard from fellow soldiers during his early days in the military. Most of them had girlfriends or wives back at home, the relationships struggling because of the deployments.

Why he had always been the go-to guy for venting about relationships, he didn't know, but he was, and because of it, he had learned quite a bit about women and the problems they caused.

It wasn't until he got back home and started talking to the Father when he realized why such problems existed. American society was to blame. It had turned its back on God. Nowhere was this more evident than in the way the modern family was structured. Men were no longer viewed as the dominant figure within the household. They had been emasculated. Many were also treated like children, ones that needed to be watched at all times or else they might accidentally destroy the house. The Father had said feminists were to blame. Josiah eventually agreed, though it pained him to do so given that it made him admit that his sister was part of the problem.

Joel had disagreed.

In fact, the mere suggestion had once angered him to the point where Josiah feared an outburst was imminent, one that would have probably gotten them kicked out of the pub they always stopped in after work.

It had shocked him.

How could Joel not see that the Father was right?

After everything his wife had put him through.

And his daughter?

I was blind, but now I see.

Such had not been the case with Joel.

No matter what Josiah did, he could not get the man to see, and the more he tried, the angrier Joel got.

Not everyone can be saved.

Josiah wished this weren't the case, but that didn't change the reality of the situation. It did make him more determined to win, though. Once this war was over, he wouldn't have to worry about losing those who could not be saved. Everyone would see the light. The world would be bathed in it to the point where denial would not be possible.

What would happen to those who were already damned?

No answer followed.

One never did.

Even the Father didn't seem to know.

In his mind, Josiah pictured Jesus throwing open the Gates of Hell and beckoning all the souls to follow him. It was a beautiful moment to visualize, one that helped cheer him on when he was at a low point, yet deep down inside, he feared it would never take place. In fact, a part of him didn't want it to take place. It wouldn't be fair. Especially to those who had led a pure life. What would they think if suddenly Hitler was allowed into Heaven after the war, his soul retrieved from the eternal torment that his earthly actions had brought upon him?

Josiah let the question fade from his mind, his focus shifting back to the task at hand.

He also reminded himself that it was not his place to question.

He could speculate, but anything beyond that was not right.

Especially now, given that he was obviously on thin ice.

THE PHONE CHARGER was on the floor behind the passenger seat, beneath an old battered gift bag that still had some ribbon on it. Four Lee Child paperback novels were inside the bag, along with a get well soon card.

Get well soon?

Curiosity piqued, he took the card with him to the driver's side of the vehicle, where he started the car and plugged in the phone.

Following that, he shifted the car into reverse and backed it up a bit so that he would have enough room to turn to the right, a realization that he could simply drive the vehicle alongside the compound fence until he came upon a copse of trees to the south having arrived while surveying the landscape.

Low fuel.

The light clicked on a few seconds after he left the road, joining a check engine light that had already been glowing, as well as a tire pressure light.

Drug addicts.

Everything around them could be crumbling, but as long as they had their fix, they wouldn't care.

It was sad.

But, alas, it was the world they lived in.

ONCE IN THE TREES, Josiah left the car running so that the phone would charge and walked back to the gate to check and see if the car was visible.

It wasn't.

Satisfied, he headed back to the car.

The get well soon card was waiting.

He opened it.

It read:

LYN,

I know things are tough right now and that the next few months will be horrible, but you have to believe that there is a light at the end of the tunnel, and once you reach it, it will welcome you into a new life that is brimming with happiness.

I love you,

Bill

PS: I don't think you've read these ones yet.

PPS: You're right, Cruise is no Reacher.

. . .

LYN? Josiah questioned.

She didn't seem like a Lyn.

But then, people sometimes didn't match up with the names their parents had chosen for them.

He had never felt like a Joseph.

All his life it had felt wrong.

The nicknames were even worse.

Especially Joey.

Ugh, growing up, his sister had frequently used that one, often exaggerating the "e" sound at the end so that she was saying, "JoEEEEEEEEEEE!"

It was like fingernails on a chalkboard.

Thankfully, the Father had fixed things.

Josiah.

It was close enough to the name Joseph that he wondered if the Lord had been trying to guide his parents into calling him Josiah. What exactly had tripped things up, he didn't know, but having been on the end of many garbled transmissions and miscommunicated orders, he did know that things like that could happen.

But from the Lord?

For a moment, he was horrified at his own implication that the Lord had failed in getting a message across, but then relaxed when he realized that Christianity itself was pretty much one long history of misinterpretation and questioning what it was that God had meant.

The fault was not with the Lord, but with man.

They could take a simple message and completely muck it up.

Some even did it on purpose, their goal being to use the message as a way to make themselves better off.

The church was a perfect example of this.

Even worse, they feared people like the Father and would do everything in their power to destroy them.

It was sad.

Christians spent so much time fighting each other that they failed to realize they were losing against the true enemy, one who was slowly but surely working its way into every aspect of society.

But that was all going to change.

The Lord had guided him to the Father, who had helped show him his purpose. And now he simply had to fulfill that purpose.

He looked at the phone.

It still had a ways to go before he could unplug it.

The Seven are in there.

He knew it.

The phone was the key.

And once he figured out who they were...

A car!

It was coming down the road toward the gate.

Josiah twisted the key, killing the engine, and then crouched down near the edge of the trees, watching.

Was this Billy?

Was he finally responding to the call the girl—Lyn—had made?

Why would it have taken so long?

He's just some dumb tweaker that I used to fuck.

A dumb tweaker who gave a gift of books and a get well soon card?

A get well soon card that talked about how the next few months would be hard, but that things would be better once they were over.

Something wasn't clicking.

He was missing something.

Something that the girl had either kept back from him or flat-out lied about.

And now he had this to deal with.

FOURTEEN

"WHAT DO you mean he isn't here?" Mel asked, dumbfounded.

"He had some personal things to attend to this morning," Dr. Fletcher's receptionist said. Her name was Jill.

"This morning," Mel noted. "It's one fifteen in the afternoon."

"I'm sorry. He isn't here."

"But I have an appointment."

Jill gave her a pained smile and said, "If you want to wait, we have lots of magazines." She motioned toward the corner where four chairs had been set up next to a small table. "Or we could reschedule."

Mel looked over at the chairs and then back at Jill, uncertainty present. "How long do you think he'll be?" she asked.

"I really can't say."

"Have you tried calling him?"

"Yes, several times, but he isn't answering his phone."

"Have you notified anyone? What if he's hurt?"

"It looks like he has an opening next Tuesday around two

thirty," Jill said, completely ignoring Mel's questions. "Should I write you in?"

"Fine, I guess—wait, Tuesday. Shit." She pulled out her phone and looked at the calendar. *Fuck!* "School starts on Tuesday."

"Oh, well, um, let's see then." She studied the appointment list. "How about Thursday at one?"

Mel stared at her.

Jill waited, eyebrows raised.

"You know what, never mind. I'll just call him myself."

"I'm sorry, I can't give out his—"

"I already have it," Mel said, cutting her off.

Jill didn't reply.

Mel used the number once she was in the hallway.

It went right to voicemail.

She didn't leave a message.

NELSON WAS WAITING for her as she stepped out of the small office complex, his body reclining on a bench near the brick walkway that led to the parking lot.

"What the fuck?" Mel demanded as he scrambled to his feet, startled by her emergence.

"Sorry, didn't mean to—" He teetered as if unable to find his balance and fell back to the bench, his right leg twisted at a horrific angle.

Mel gasped.

Nelson cursed.

"Are you—" she started.

He pulled up his pant leg.

Mel's eyes went wide.

"It has felt off all morning, but I couldn't figure out what it was," he said, fingers pulling back a thin sleeve and then unclipping two straps. "It just wasn't sitting right." He examined it for a second and then shook his head. "Huh."

"What happened?" Mel asked.

"Mortar round. Came out of nowhere and landed square in our FOB while I was heading to a chow line." He shook his head. "A week before I was going home."

"That sucks."

He looked up at her for a moment and then laughed.

"What?" she asked.

"Most people don't react like that," he said, grinning. "It's refreshing."

"Ohhhkayyy," she said and started to walk toward her car.

"Whoa, hold up."

"I don't think so," she said, though she did slow her steps.

"Please, I didn't mean to startle you."

She turned and glared at him.

"Honestly," he added.

Every ounce of good sense that she possessed was telling her to continue walking, and had he not been standing there holding a prosthetic leg in one hand while balanced on his remaining leg, she would have.

"Do you know how creepy it is for me to leave my doctor's office and see you sitting there waiting for me?" she asked.

"Sorry," he said.

"I mean, shit, the mall was bad enough, but now this"—she waved her hands—"this is legit stalking."

"I'm just looking out for you."

"He's not going to come after me," she snapped.

He didn't reply.

"Seriously," she added.

"You don't know that," he said, voice solemn.

He's right, she said to herself.

"Something triggered all of this, something that hasn't been resolved yet," he continued.

"He was after my father, not me," she said.

"Yeah, so why not kill you too and simply be done with it?" he asked. "Why did he hold on to you the way he did?"

She didn't reply.

"And why did he kill your father?" he asked. "Has anyone figured that out yet?"

She stared.

"There's more to this than meets the eye," he added.

"Yeah," she agreed, voice barely audible. "But what?"

"I don't know, but I'd like to find out."

"Why?"

The doors to the main entrance opened, two women stepping out, their business-suit-clad bodies stopping as they saw Nelson standing in the middle of the walkway, holding his prosthetic leg.

"Either of you ladies have any duct tape?" Nelson asked.

"Um...no," one of them said, startled.

The other actually checked her purse but then shook her head while muttering an apology.

"It's okay," Nelson said. "I'll hop on home and grab some."

Mel had to cover a smile as the two women tried to figure out the proper reply.

Once they left, Nelson returned to the bench and pulled a small tool kit from his pocket, his fingers using an Allen wrench to make some adjustments before addressing the straps and then securing everything back in place.

He stood.

"Is it okay?" Mel asked.

"Eh..." he said, giving a so-so wave. "I supposedly have a new one in the works, but with the VA, who knows when that will arrive."

"I hear they're pretty horrible."

"That's putting it nicely." He took a test step. "They fucking suck."

Mel waited.

He took another step. "With my luck, it will finally arrive, only it will be the wrong leg."

"No!" Mel said, putting a hand to her mouth. "Does that really happen?"

"It wouldn't surprise me." He took another step. "Actually though, the VA isn't really involved in this with me anymore. They were at first, but I got so frustrated dealing with them that I finally jumped ship and went private. GoFundMe, *woo-hoo!* When I do have to call them about various things...ugh, it's unbelievably bad. I'd rather swim through the colon of a constipated whale than be on the phone with them trying to get through to someone who knows what the fuck they're doing."

Mel snorted and then felt her face flush.

"So," Nelson asked, thumb pointing over his shoulder toward the doors, "what's the deal with Dr. Fletcher? Normally you wouldn't be out until two."

"Jesus, creeper alert," Mel said, voice hinting at humor.

"Sorry."

"Seriously, how do you know that's who I've been seeing?"

"It actually wasn't all that difficult to find out."

She crossed her arms and waited.

"This place has three doctors. One has been on vacation, so you obviously weren't seeing him. The other posted tons of photos of himself at a fancy party on a fancy paddleboat on the Mississippi during the eclipse, so you obviously weren't seeing him. And then there was Dr. Fletcher."

Mel stared at him for several seconds.

"It's kind of frightening, really, all the information that is available with just a few clicks of a mouse. People have no idea just how visible their lives are in this digital era."

Mel didn't know what to say to that.

"And if I could figure this out, so could Joe, which is why I think you should really be a bit more cautious."

"Okay, point taken."

Nelson eyed her for a moment and then nodded.

"You hungry?" Mel asked.

"Yeah, I could eat," Nelson confirmed.

"Good, because I missed lunch and now could really go for a burger, your treat."

"My treat?"

"Yep.

"Where at?" he asked.

"What? And let you lose your mad stalker skills. No way." With that, she twisted around toward the parking lot and headed to her car.

"MY GOD, I thought these all went out of business," Nelson said.

"What? Why'd you think that?"

"Because the one by my parents' place went away while I was overseas. It actually was a little heartbreaking because it was one of those places that we used to go to for my birthday parties when I was a kid. Getting to build your own burger was pretty epic in those days. Plus, kids always got a free cookie from the dessert bar. You could refill your Coke all you wanted. And they had a good Ninja Turtles arcade, which was so much better than the NES One game."

Mel stared at him for several seconds and then asked, "Do you need a moment, or can we go in and get some burgers?"

Nelson gave her a look and then said, "After you."

"NO NINJA TURTLES ARCADE," Mel said as they

secured a table in the far corner of the restaurant, near some windows that looked out at the parking lot.

"Oh well, some things are best left as fond memories since trying to relive those memories can bring about disappointment rather than enjoyment."

Mel didn't reply to that.

"I learned that the hard way when watching *Three Ninjas* a while back," he added.

"*Three Ninjas*?"

Yep. When that came out, I thought it was the greatest movie of all time. My poor parents. I probably dragged them to it ten times before it finally left theaters."

"Jesus, you saw that when it came out?"

"Yep."

"I didn't realize you were so old."

"Old? I'm thirty-five."

"Newsflash, that's old."

He laughed and then twisted as his name was called over the microphone. "That's us."

Together they started toward the counter, but then Mel stopped and said, "Oops, forgot my glass," and hurried back to the table, where she quickly took out her phone and snapped a picture of Nelson's car through the window.

A minute later, she was grabbing her burger from the counter, one that she overloaded with tomatoes, lettuce, onions, pickles, ketchup, mustard, and mayo.

Nelson only put mayo on his.

"All these toppings to choose from and that's all you're going with?" Mel asked.

"What can I say, I'm a simple man with simple tastes."

"Whatever."

Burgers in hand, they headed back to the table, Mel stopping to fill her glass with some Cherry Coke.

Nelson waited for her to take her seat before taking a bite

of his burger, his eyes rolling back into his head as he overly exaggerated the pleasure the food brought to him.

Mel followed suit, satisfaction present as she chewed her food, though it had nothing to do with the taste. Instead, she was proud of herself for securing a photo of his license plate. How exactly she would learn anything from it was a mystery, but just having it felt like a good thing since something seemed off about Nelson. She couldn't put her finger on what it was exactly, but it was certainly there, lingering within her mind.

"SO, TELL ME MORE ABOUT HIM," Mel said as they finished their burgers. "What was he like before he was burned?"

"Quiet. Reserved. Some would say shy, but he wasn't. It just appeared that way because he didn't feel the need to jump into every conversation. He also didn't really have much in common with the other guys on his team. He wasn't an outcast or anything; he just didn't share the same interests as they did."

"What were his interests?" Mel asked.

"No one really knew."

"Was he religious?"

Nelson considered that for several seconds before saying, "Not really. He wasn't an atheist or anything, but he didn't carry the Lord with him everywhere he went. No Bible that I ever saw, no real religious preference when Christmas rolled around. In fact, he didn't really seem all that upset to be spending Christmas away from home, which was odd. Even the most hardened soldier got a bit down when the holidays rolled around."

"And yet he formed a bond with a priest in the old folks' home."

"Being wounded changes things."

"Did he seem religious after that?"

"I really don't know."

"Why not?"

"We weren't able to visit him after he was medevaced out of there. Not with the risk of infection from the burns. And then, once they were able to get him stable, he was flown to Germany and then back to the States, where he spent a long time undergoing skin grafts and physical therapy."

"And you never tried to get in touch with him at all, even after you were back?"

"I kind of had my own recovery to focus on." He studied a fry for a moment but then tossed it back into the basket. "Learning to walk again with a prosthetic is not an easy feat. It's only been during the last two months where I've felt comfortable enough to venture out on my own."

"Oh."

"And now that I am confident enough to walk around on my own, all this happens." He shook his head. "A day late and a dollar short."

Several seconds came and went.

"Do you really think you could have prevented all this?" Mel asked.

"I don't know. Maybe."

"How?"

A shrug was his only reply.

Several more seconds came and went.

"Something happened," Mel said. "With him and that priest."

"What was it?"

"I don't know, but I think it upset my father."

"How so?"

Mel told him what she had learned during her visit to the old folks' home.

"Oh shit, sounds like your father may have thought he had a breakthrough in the works, only to find out something else was unfolding, something that he must have put a sudden stop to, which upset Joe."

"So much so that he would kill my father?"

"Apparently." He sipped his Coke. "Did your father keep notes on what unfolded? Or a recording? Anything?"

"He must have, but I haven't been able to find it."

"Hmm."

"I think Ms. Hayden has them," she said.

"Ms. Hayden?" he asked.

"At the old folks' home. She was kind of in charge of everything, publicity wise."

"And what, you think she hid the notes?"

Mel nodded and then said, "From what she said, it seems like what my father was doing wasn't really proper, and now with what happened, I think she's worried about it coming to light and ruining her career."

"Ah, blowback."

"Blowback?"

He waved her question away and said, "Here's the one issue I have with that. Would she really have hid this potential evidence from the police after your father was murdered and you disappeared? Long before the shooting during the eclipse?"

"For sure."

"But why? The shooting is what drew everyone's attention to the old folks' home. Hiding or even destroying his notes before that wouldn't make any sense."

"But it does," Mel said. "Think about it. What if she originally hid the notes simply because she didn't think anything within them really applied to my father being murdered, so she figured why draw attention to the unorthodox sessions my father was conducting with the priest and Joe when all it could do was hurt her career and the old folks' home? But then, *boom*, it turns out it was all connected and now she realizes she not only hid evidence, but now could be blamed for allowing the shooting to happen. After all, if she had shown the police the notes, they might have gone to question Joe, and then found me and then arrested him before he shot up the place."

"Okay," Nelson said, enthusiasm showing. "That actually sounds pretty legit."

"So, what do we do?"

"It's simple," he said with a grin. "We ask her for the notes."

FIFTEEN

JOSIAH HIT the Send button on the phone in his right hand while watching the phone in his left. It didn't ring or buzz or make any indication whatsoever that the call from the one in his right was being received by the one in his left.

He ended the call.

The man on the ground was not Billy.

He had already been pretty certain of this given the driver's license he had pulled from the man's wallet, but then realized the man might have used an alias while talking to Lyn.

Unless he has a second phone...

A drug pusher would probably do that. Especially if he was leading a double life. Respectable looking on one side, despicable on the other.

Then again, the girl had said that Billy was a tweaker.

This man didn't look like a tweaker.

He had seemed healthy, his face plump and full of life. And there were no marks on his arms that would indicate needle use.

Lyn gets drugs from Billy, who gets them from...

That had to be it.

Billy had called this guy about Lyn, who had gotten concerned because he had probably been the one to send the three out here in hopes of locating a new location for cooking meth.

But why come alone?

If he was some heavy-duty drug dealer, wouldn't he have men to do this stuff for him?

Josiah thought about this for several seconds and then shook the question away. He didn't know enough about the drug trade to come to any meaningful conclusions. Plus, he now had another vehicle to deal with, and a body to dispose of.

A HALF HOUR LATER, Josiah was walking back to the compound, the body of Charles Fletcher having gone into the trunk of the first car while the vehicle he had arrived in was parked next to it within the copse of trees, ready to be used should he need to take it anywhere or make any type of retreat from the compound.

Retreat.

The word stuck in his mind.

He had no fallback position.

And even if he did, both vehicles were in a location that would be difficult to escape from because if the authorities did descend upon the compound in force, the main road in would almost certainly be used as a staging area.

Would they have air support?

To prevent his escape?

Drones?

Choppers?

If so, a vehicle would become a death trap because tracking it as he fled would be simple. Going on foot wouldn't be much better, especially with the girl.

Retreat would not be an option.

If push came to shove, he would have to make a stand.

But to what end?

Was his only task to be the elimination of the Seven?

Once that was completed, would he be relieved of his duty?

No.

It seemed like there should be more.

Once the Seven were gone, new threats would appear, ones that he would need to protect her from.

Focus!

The Seven were the priority.

Worrying about future missions was pointless. Dangerous too, because it could become a distraction.

Like Iraq.

The overall mission in Afghanistan had suffered considerably once the focus had shifted. So much so that all these years later, it was still being pursued.

Blue eyes.

Tiny body.

Screams.

Fire!

Josiah ground his teeth together against the pain that flared, his body almost able to feel the flames cooking his flesh.

Deep breath!

Another.

And another.

Several seconds came and went, his mind unable to shake the pain, his hands actually patting himself in an attempt to smother the flames that he could feel but not see.

Tears appeared.

He let them fall.

They didn't last long, and once they stopped he took a final deep breath and continued his journey back into the compound, the gift bag and card in one hand, the girl's phone in the other.

Why he carried the phone he didn't know. He could have put it in his pocket. Carry it he did though, almost as if he wanted to be ready should it ring.

THE GIRL DIDN'T KNOW who Charles Fletcher was, but admitted that she might have fucked him for smack at some point.

"How would he know to come here?" Josiah asked, voice struggling to stay calm.

She shrugged.

"Would Billy have told him where you were?"

Another shrug.

Josiah shook his head and started to leave, but then stopped and said, "You're a Jack Reacher fan?"

She lifted her head, a startled look on her face.

He waited.

"No," she said.

It was a pointless lie, which irked him.

"I found a gift bag in your car with four books in it," he said. "From Billy."

She stared at him.

"And a get well soon card," he added.

Her lower lip began to quiver, and without warning she burst into tears.

Surprised, Josiah stepped back.

"I ruined it," she said between sobs, voice wet with tears and snot.

"Ruined what?" he asked.

"Everything!" she cried, body sagging against the handcuffs.

Josiah didn't know how to reply to that, so he simply stood there, waiting, shifting himself from one foot to another.

"Did he send you?" she asked after nearly five minutes, her sobs finally stalling out.

"Who?"

She wiped her face against her left shoulder, smearing the snot and tears. "Billy?"

"Billy?"

"To punish me."

"Punish you? No. I'm here to protect you."

"He sent you to protect me?"

"Billy didn't send me," he said.

She waited, face making a second pass against her shoulder.

"God sent me."

Her eyes widened. "God sent you?"

"Yes," he confirmed.

She stared at him for a long time and then burst out laughing.

"You're fucking insane," she said, fresh tears appearing.

Sticks and stones...

"I'm not," he replied, voice wavering. "God sent me to protect you from the Seven."

"Jesus Christ—"

He backhanded her, the blow splitting her lip but doing nothing to stop the laugher.

Don't! a voice warned as he nearly struck her again.

Guilt followed.

Disappointment too.

He had lost his cool.

"Did God tell you to do that?" she taunted, blood dripping from her chin.

Josiah took a deep breath and turned to leave.

"I bet he'll tell you to fuck me too!"

He stepped from the room.

"In my tight little pussy and then up my ass. Jesus loves seeing me fucked in—"

He closed the door, shutting off her voice, leaving her in darkness once again.

THE MAN whose finger he had broken earlier started shaking as soon as Josiah appeared, an undecipherable plea echoing from his dry lips.

"I have some questions," Josiah said, a calmness having returned during his journey from the subterranean areas to the main floor.

"O-o-kay," the man sputtered.

"Any hesitation in answering them, and I'll break a finger."

The man began to cry.

Josiah shook his head and said, "Stop."

The man didn't.

Josiah took hold of a finger.

The crying was replaced by a whimper.

"Why did you three come here?" Josiah asked.

"W-we needed a place to crash," the man said.

"Who sent you?"

"N-no o-one."

A shriek echoed as his finger snapped.

"Who sent you!" Josiah demanded.

"No one!"

Josiah squeezed the two broken fingers together.

"No one! *No one! No one! PLEASE!*"

Josiah released the finger.

"Who's Charles Fletcher?"

Panic appeared in the man's eyes.

"Are you hesitating?" Josiah asked, taking hold of another finger.

The man pissed himself.

"I don't know!"

"Don't know what?"

"I don't know that name!"

"What's the girl's name?"

"Madalyn."

"Madalyn?" he asked.

"Yes."

"But she goes by Lyn?"

"Yes."

"Why did you bring her here?"

"She wanted to come here."

"She did?"

"Yes!"

"Why?"

"To crash."

"Were you going to have sex with her?"

Hesitation.

Snap.

Scream.

"Yes! She owes us!"

"Are you one of the Seven?"

No answer.

Josiah grabbed a finger.

"Wait!"

"Are you one of the Seven?"

"Seven what?"

Josiah snapped the finger and then squeezed all of them together, grinding them.

Nothing but screams followed, and then sobs, and finally heaves as the man started to vomit.

Josiah backed off.

Nothing but tiny strands of stomach acid came up, most of it now dangling from the man's chin.

Five minutes came and went.

"Once all your fingers are broken, I'll start pulling finger-nails," he said.

"Please."

"Tell me about the Seven."

"I don't know who they are."

"But you know of them?" Josiah asked.

Hesitation and then, "Y-yes."

"Tell me about them," Josiah instructed.

"I don't know much."

"Tell me what you know."

The man blinked and asked for water.

Josiah gave him some and then waited.

"Alec knows more than me about the Seven, but I—"

"Alec?" Josiah asked, cutting him off.

"Lyn's friend. I don't know him too well, but he always has good glass. That's why I tagged along."

"Glass?"

"Ice."

"Ice?"

"Crystal."

"Meth?"

"Yes."

"Where can I find him?"

"Did he get away?"

It clicked.

"The other one is named Alec?"

"Yes! And he knows all about the Seven."

Josiah left the room and hurried to where the other man was.

Nothing needed to be broken before Alec decided to tell Josiah what he knew about the Seven. Names were confirmed, Josiah reading from the list in Lyn's contacts while Alec said either yes or no.

Billy was not one of the names.

Josiah asked about this.

"Billy?" the man questioned, exhaustion straining his voice. "Shit, man, you don't want to mess with Billy. He'll fuck you up."

"But he's not one of the Seven?"

"Dude, they'd all shit bricks if they knew he was gunning for them."

Josiah didn't know what to make of this.

"What about you?" Josiah asked. "Would you shit bricks too if he was after you?"

"Fuck, man, why do you think we came all the way out here to hide?"

"You're hiding from Billy?"

"Yeah, man, he'll fucking kill us if he finds us."

"Why?"

"Go ask Lyn. She's the reason we're all in this mess."

"I'm asking you," Josiah said, stepping forward. He cracked his knuckles.

"Shit, man, okay, okay," Alec cried. "He was going to force her into rehab, but we bailed her out."

"Rehab," Josiah muttered to himself, the get well soon card suddenly making sense. "He's trying to help her?"

"Yeah," Alec laughed. "And best of all, she swiped his debit card so we were able to score big time before coming out here. We hit every ATM we could find before the sun was even up and then she sucked us both off."

He was trying to help her and these two prevented it.

Was that why the Lord had led them here?

So I can stop these two from completely ruining her and get her back to rehab?

But what about the Seven?

"Nothing like a blowjob to start the day," Alec continued.

Josiah's attention shifted back to the man, anger warming his blood.

Whoever Billy was, he had been doing the Lord's work, which meant this guy was doing the opposite.

Alec's laugher stopped, concern appearing.

Josiah stepped toward him.

"Whoa, man, what's up?"

"You made her suck your dick even though she gave you tons of money from Billy's debit card?" Josiah questioned.

"Yeah, man, but she, like, owed us."

"Owed you?" Josiah demanded and then drove a knee up into the man's testicles. "Sounds like you owe her."

A weak gasp was all that followed, the ropes making it so Alec could not collapse to the ground the way his body wanted.

Josiah hit him two more times and then, just to be sure the damage was enough, reached into the pervert's pants and squeezed the sweaty testicles until he felt a pop within his grip.

No screams echoed, Alec having lost consciousness during the squeeze.

The same could not be said of the other man.

Ten minutes later, his screams were still bouncing around within Josiah's head as he contemplated his next steps.

Call Billy?

Let him bring her to rehab?

Or simply let her get clean here?

Either way the outcome would be the same.

Billy might not see me as being helpful...

And the Seven are still out there.

These two perverts weren't even a part of the Seven, yet they had already caused quite a bit of trouble for Lyn. Knowing that, there was no telling how much worse the Seven would be.

No.

He needed to eliminate that threat before he allowed Lyn to leave the compound. She wouldn't like it, but sometimes that was life.

After all, he hadn't liked burning off his tattoos, especially his Special Forces one, but that had been part of the cleansing process.

Joel hadn't liked that.

That had been the moment things changed.

Josiah hadn't planned on telling him about the act, but the wound had started to ooze, the seepage soaking through the bandage and his shirt. Once Joel saw that—once he realized that Josiah was actually performing the acts the Father had insisted upon during their talks—it had been the beginning of the end. Try as he might, he could not get his friend to understand. Nothing got through to him.

He sighed.

Not everyone was ready.

It was like that movie with the hacker that he had seen with his sister while they had been in high school, the one where everyone was living in a computer-generated fantasy world. The name escaped him, as did many memories from that period, but he did recall one character telling the other that not everyone was ready to be saved and because of that, they might need to be eliminated, given that the enemy could use them.

SIXTEEN

"YOU CAN'T BE SERIOUS," Mel said.

"What?" Nelson questioned. "I'm totally serious."

"You can't just go there and demand the notes."

"Why not?"

"Because she'll probably call the cops."

"And risk them finding out that she hid evidence from them?" He shook his head. "Nah, I don't think so."

"But we don't even know if she really has them."

"You seemed pretty sure a second ago."

"Yeah, but..." Mel couldn't really think up a way to counter that. "I just don't know."

"Hey, it's cool. We'll put that on the back burner for now."

Back burner.

Shit.

He was viewing them as some sort of team now.

She didn't like that.

Yet at the same time, he seemed to want what she wanted: answers.

But why?

What did he hope to gain by getting answers?

What do I hope to gain?

She didn't really have an answer for either question.

If asked, she would have claimed closure, but deep down inside she knew that would never really arrive.

"What is it?" Nelson asked.

"Nothing," she said with a wave of her hand.

"Nothing?"

"Nothing," she insisted, voice a bit more forceful.

"Okay," he said, holding up his hands.

She stared at him.

He stared back.

"You're going to go try and strong-arm her, aren't you?" Mel said.

"Eh, I don't know if 'strong-arm' is the right phrase."

"Well, you're certainly not going to charm it from her."

"Gee, thanks." He stood up.

"Whoa. What're you doing?"

"Heading to the old folks' home so I can try to strong-arm her." He finished his soda with a long chug and set the empty glass down on the table.

Mel held up a hand while standing. "No, no, I really don't think—"

"Hey, relax," he said, cutting her off with a chuckle. "I'm not going anywhere near the old folks' home. I said we'll back-burner that idea, and that's what I'm doing."

"Oh."

"But I do have to get going. Here's my number if you need anything." He wrote it down on a napkin. "Or if you think of anything."

"Okay," she said, looking at it.

She didn't offer hers, and he didn't ask.

Does he already have it?

Did he figure that out through all his social media snooping?

The thought produced a chill.

She had always known her info was out there. One couldn't get by without their data becoming a part of the web. But she hadn't realized just how easily it could be used to deduce things about her.

If he can do it, I can do it.

This thought stuck with her during the short drive home, her mind envisioning herself pulling up tons of information on Nelson and using it to figure out everything she needed to know about him and his motivations in seeking her out.

Nothing.

She couldn't even find a Facebook profile, at least not one that looked like it belonged to him. The name was too generic and brought about too many results.

Google was no better.

Even adding things like "wounded," "Afghanistan," "one leg," and "special forces" didn't produce anything that was useful to her.

And the photo of his license plate didn't help.

Typing the number itself into the search box brought up results, but none of them were about him. At least, none of the ones she looked at were, and she wasn't about to click through the million plus links that Google found just on the chance that something about him would pop up.

Frustrated, she pushed away from her computer and headed down into the family room to check out Netflix, the peace and quiet of a motherless house something she didn't get to enjoy all that often.

Nothing new was on that she wanted to watch, so she started revisiting old shows that she had previously enjoyed, but nothing could keep her attention, her finger constantly starting and stopping the programs.

And then something clicked.

If Nelson had used Facebook to learn about her sessions

with Dr. Fletcher, then that meant he had to have a Facebook profile, one that she could simply ask him about rather than trying to seek it out. After all, it seemed like he wanted to partner up with her, so why not make their connection official via a Facebook friendship?

Phone in hand, she typed up a text letting him know he should send her a friend request.

Following that, she waited.

And waited.

And waited.

He wasn't reading the text.

She considered calling him, but then thought better of it and set her phone back down.

Less than a minute later, it rang.

It was Dr. Fletcher.

"Hello?" she asked.

Nothing.

"Hello?"

Still nothing, though she could hear stuff in the background.

Butt dial?

The longer she listened, the more she realized this had to be the case.

Concern followed.

He wasn't answering his phone, but it was obviously on.

What did that mean?

It means nothing.

He probably just needed a break.

But a break from what?

And why not let everyone know?

If he had canceled his appointments for the day, she wouldn't have given things a second thought. Instead, he had left everyone hanging, and that just didn't seem like him.

Something was up.

Something that he hadn't expected to take him away from his afternoon appointments.

Joseph?

Would he have gone after him to get at her?

Could he have?

Finding his address wouldn't have been all that difficult. One didn't even have to be a social media wizard to do so. Simply following him home from his office would have done the trick.

But first one would have to know that was who she had been seeing, which meant one did have to be a bit of a social media wizard.

Give it a try.

Nelson had pretty much spelled out his steps in how he had figured out she was doing sessions with Dr. Fletcher. By following what he did, she might glean something useful.

What exactly that usefulness might be, she didn't know, but at least it would feel like she was doing something.

She called Dr. Fletcher while heading back up to her computer, just to see if he would notice the ringing of his phone and answer.

Voicemail.

Again.

This time she left a message, one that needlessly noted he had missed their appointment and that she hoped everything was okay. The latter statement was actually true. It didn't happen often, but she had started to feel a bond developing with Dr. Fletcher, one that she never would have imagined possible a few weeks earlier when contemplating her first visit with the shrink.

FRUSTRATED, Mel pushed away from her computer desk, her attempt at following the steps Nelson had taken in figuring out which doctor she was seeing having failed. Finding the profiles of the two doctors was not a problem, but finding the pictures and information that Nelson had mentioned was impossible. It just wasn't there. She had spent an hour scouring each profile, all to no avail.

If the mentioned photos were real, they were visible to friends only, and since Nelson was not a friend of either doctor —she had studied both lists carefully—there was no way he could have seen them and used the information to track down Dr. Fletcher.

He lied.

It was either that or all the info he had used had suddenly been switched over to "friends only" by both of the doctors.

Yeah, right.

If one or two photos had been switched over, then she would consider it a possibility, but every single item that Nelson had mentioned...no way.

He had lied to her.

But why?

What was he hiding?

She stared at her computer screen while asking herself this, her mind trying to think up a way to use the machine to find answers. Something had to be in there, something that was lurking within the tangled web of cyberspace, quietly waiting for the right search string to pull it up.

Or was it?

Dr. Fletcher had warned her that in an attempt to find meaning within the events that had unfolded she might create complexities that weren't really there.

"*Sometimes we have to simply accept the fact that shit happens,*" he had said.

Shit happens.

She didn't want to accept that.

Couldn't accept it.

Not yet.

Not after learning about the connection between her father, Joseph, and the former priest. And not with Nelson out there.

Something was going on, something that she had gotten caught up in.

Shit happens might have defined her entry into the mess, but it no longer could be used to dismiss everything that had followed.

Nelson's entry proved this.

Would Dr. Fletcher agree?

She pictured him in his chair, contemplating her vocalized thoughts, a gentle nod followed by a statement that would be vague enough to show that he wasn't committing to a yes or no, but instead thought Nelson's entry into the situation was intriguing.

A realization that she was longing for that look of contemplation arrived, a longing that went beyond her current thoughts and was simply a general need for his presence.

Talking with him helped.

It didn't matter what it was they discussed, just the interaction that took place during the forty-five minutes of time every week seemed to act as a balm upon her mind.

And now she didn't have that.

A buzz echoed from her phone.

She picked it up.

Nelson.

The message read: *FB profile? Sure. Coming right up.*

She waited, her eyes staring at the dot bubble that wobbled beneath his previous message.

A minute came and went, and then another.

The dot bubble disappeared.

A link appeared.

She clicked it.

It brought her to the main page of Facebook.

She shook her head and typed up a message that read: *Try again. That just brought me to the main page.*

What? he replied. *Okay, one sec.*

A new link appeared.

She clicked it.

Main page again, she replied.

Fuck.

A dot bubble followed.

Third time the charm? she asked herself.

Nope.

A link did not follow. Instead, he wrote: *I can't seem to do this from my phone. I'll have to do it from my computer once I get back to my motel.*

Okay, she replied.

A thumbs-up emoji followed.

She sighed.

Wait a second!

She typed: *Why don't you simply send me a friend request?*

Nothing followed. No dot bubble, no message, no Read at...nothing.

She set her phone back down, her mind unsure what to think.

Something was off about Nelson. Of this she had no doubt. But what it was exactly, she couldn't pinpoint.

HOLY SHIT!

Dr. Fletcher was gay.

She had had no idea, which was why she was shocked. She had always assumed she would be able to tell. Especially in this day and age, when one no longer had to hide it.

He isn't hiding it, she noted to herself, one simple Facebook click having revealed it. Yet even so, he seemed so...not gay.

The same was true of his partner.

Neither one fit what she had always envisioned. In fact, if the two had not been listed as being married to one another on Facebook, she would never have known.

Wow. Just wow.

A moment later, she sent a message, one that stated she was a patient of Dr. Fletcher and was concerned because he hadn't shown up for their appointment that day.

She wasn't exactly sure what the message would accomplish, if anything, but no other ideas were forthcoming.

To her surprise, a reply arrived within seconds.

It simply read: *Call me, please,* and provided a phone number.

Startled, she picked up her phone and punched in the number, but then hesitated before hitting Send.

Too forward.

He's worried.

Still...

Fuck it.

She hit Send.

"Do you know where he is?" a frantic voice demanded as soon as the call connected.

"Whoa, no. I was hoping you could tell me. Is he okay?"

"I don't know. He said he was going to check out something up north before his sessions. And now he isn't returning calls and no one has heard anything from him."

"Up north?" she asked, the panic within his voice causing her own heart to race. "What's up north?"

"I don't know," he nearly cried. "Something about a straitjacket."

"A straitjacket?"

"Yes! He's been obsessed. Doing research into all hours of the night. Making calls. Grumbling about the police."

"Why?"

"I don't know! I figured you would know."

"Me?"

"Yes. It's all about you and the straitjacket."

"I don't..." He had been curious about it, especially after the detectives had burst into their first session.

"You don't what?" he asked.

"I don't know. We talked about the straitjacket a bit early on, but I had no idea he was doing research into it."

"This is so like him. He doesn't tell anyone anything."

"And he didn't tell you where he was going?"

"No! Just that he had to check something out up north."

"How far up north?"

"I don't know!"

"It must not have been too far since he didn't cancel any of his sessions."

"That's what I said, but the police don't think it's a big deal."

"You've spoken to the police?"

"Yes. And they won't do anything."

"And he spoke to the police too?"

"What?"

"You said he was grumbling about the police."

"Oh, yes. He complained they wouldn't take him seriously."

"Do you know what he had told them?"

"No, just that he was upset because they started calling him Jessica."

"Jessica?"

"As in Jessica Fletcher."

"Who?"

"*Murder, She Wrote.*"

"What's that?"

"Never mind." Exhaustion was suddenly present in his voice.

"Did he have notes, something that might show where he was going?"

"Do you think I'd be this freaked out if I knew where he was?" he snapped.

"Jeez. I'm just trying to help."

"But you're not. No one is." Then, more to himself, "Why does he do this?"

Mel didn't have an answer for him and decided to end the call, a pointless statement on how she would see if she could figure out where he went and let him know leaving her lips.

A thankless "thanks" echoed in her ear.

Mel shook her head, but then shifted her focus.

Straitjacket.

Something up north.

What in the world had he been looking into?

Nothing popped into her mind.

They really hadn't spent much time talking about the straitjacket. In fact, this was the first she had thought about it since he had asked her a few questions during her second visit a few weeks earlier—questions that had seemed pointless.

"How thick was it? Did it seem heavy or lightweight? What were the buckles like? Did the material have any give? Did you notice a manufacture mark?"

After a while she had jokingly asked him if he had a straitjacket fetish that he was getting off on.

"No, no," he had said with a laugh. *"Just trying to get a feel for the situation."*

A lie.

One that she had believed.

But now...

What had he been up to?

What was up north that had piqued his interest?

And why didn't he tell anyone about it?

He did, and then complained that the police wouldn't take him seriously.

Call them.

Find out what he told them.

She pulled out the card that Detective Higgins had slipped her after her first interview with them, one that she had told him she would throw out as soon as she left the station but had actually tucked into the sleeve on her phone case once she was out of sight.

Hesitation hit.

Anger too.

They hadn't believed her when she first told the story of her ordeal, Detective Simmons going so far as to imply that she had staged everything.

And he wasn't the only one.

Many in the media had come to this conclusion as well, likely because her mother had casually mentioned to the press that her tale did seem a bit embellished. She had then gone on to add that this embellishment was likely due to her mind not being able to cope with the reality of the ordeal and thus creating one that was easier for her to tolerate.

Only the first part of the statement was used in the headlines and sound bites, something that her mother acted dismayed about even though she should have known better. Even after her claims were confirmed, the media and police still seemed skeptical of her.

"*It's hard to admit to a mistake,*" Dr. Fletcher had said. "*Once we form an opinion on something or someone, it's almost impossible to change it.*"

"*Even if all the evidence points toward their opinion being wrong?*" Mel had asked.

"*All the evidence almost makes it worse, because then we*

entrench ourselves in the belief and seek out ways to confirm it, which often leads to digging up sources that are suspect at best."

"Like vaccines and autism?"

"Exactly."

Mel pondered this for a while, her mind dancing around the idea that she might have fallen victim to this as well in regards to Detective Simmons and Higgins.

No, not Simmons. He was a chauvinistic pig. But Higgins...?

She shifted her attention back to the card he had given her, one that had his cell number written on the back.

At the time she had seen this gesture as part of an elaborate good cop, bad cop routine, but now she wondered...maybe it wasn't a routine. Maybe one truly was a good cop, while the other was a bad cop.

Call him and find out.

She picked up her phone and thumbed in the numbers.

SEVENTEEN

JOSIAH HAD the names of the Seven, but no addresses. Why Lyn had not bothered to fill those in, he did not know, and she was not forthcoming with the information when asked. She didn't even want to admit that she knew who the Seven were, her face one of dismay when he mentioned them and the names.

Practiced dismay.

The girl was good, but not good enough to fool him.

She knew who the Seven were.

Now the question was, how would he get the rest of their info?

Fingers?

No.

He didn't want to hurt her. Couldn't hurt her. Just seeing the dried blood on her lip as she dangled in the restraints pained him.

Let her down.

It will help in building trust.

The inner voice was his own, but the words were not. He was being guided. Instructed.

He did not obey. Could not. Without the restraints, there was no way she would stay in the old closet, the latch that secured the door to the wall having long since broken free.

Indecision gripped him.

Other rooms were available, some padded, others simply ones where patients had been housed. A few even had beds still, though the mattresses had seen better days.

Trouble was, most of those rooms no longer had doors, and the ones that did wouldn't stay closed since the handles had all been removed. It was odd, almost as if someone had come through and taken them.

Why?

Were they valuable?

Or had it been done as a safety precaution?

He wandered the halls while thinking about this, his eyes on the lookout for anything that might help him latch the door so that he could let her down as instructed.

Nothing was jumping out at him.

His only other option was to put her into one of the strait-jackets that he had found several months earlier in one of the storage rooms, but he worried that given the nimbleness she had displayed earlier, she would be able to wiggle her way out.

Focus on the Seven.

Once they were eliminated, he could start trying to build trust with Lyn.

But without trust, she won't give you the information you need to find them.

Unless...

He pulled out the phone and thumbed open the contact info for the first of the names that Alec had confirmed was a member of the Seven.

Text him.

See if he'll give up his address.

All he needed was one, and then the rest would be within his grasp.

Maybe not right away, but once he started inflicting pain, information would be provided. It always was. He had learned this while watching some of the agency people in Afghanistan. The black sites were off-limits, but one didn't need to be on a black site to see the agency people extracting information. They would simply do it out in the field, when they had low-level terrorists in hand, ones that weren't valuable enough to bring back after the mission ended. Instead, info would be extracted and then they would be eliminated. A simple casualty of the engagement.

A scream echoed, one that he could not block out given that it came from within his own mind.

Blue eyes.

Soft skin.

Perfect breasts.

Tears.

Shrieks!

Grunts!

Fire!

No! No! No!

He clutched his face, and when that didn't work, he punched the wall with his free hand.

Pain erupted, but at least the memory faded.

But for how long?

They're getting more frequent.

No, they're not.

Yes, they are.

The first voice was right: they were getting more frequent. And more debilitating.

But why?

Stress?

The girl?

The Seven?

All of the above?

Talking to the Father had always helped. Far more than the army shrink they had forced him to see for several months while in Germany.

But now he had no one.

The thought saddened him a bit as he headed back to the main room, his right hand cradled against his stomach as he walked.

It was tough being a chosen one.

Loneliness was always a factor.

Even the prophets of old had faced it, and back then people were more willing to believe in the idea of one being chosen and spoken to by God. Now...well...it was almost fitting that he was wandering the halls of an old mental institution because if he wasn't in this one, society probably would have found a different one for him to reside in.

A BUZZING SOUND caught his attention as he sat in the main room bandaging his hand, the punch to the wall having broken his right ring finger.

Charles Fletcher's phone.

He had set it on one of the old MRE boxes earlier and now it was dancing across the surface with a call, butting up against the wallet and keys he had retrieved from the dead man's pockets.

The buzzing stopped.

Josiah finished bandaging his hand and then went over to the phone to see who it was that had called.

One of the Seven?

Nope.

Louis.

He didn't think he had seen that one yet, but just to be sure, he opened up Lyn's phone and checked the contacts.

No Louis.

And yet Louis had called several times it seemed, a note showing that this was the fifth missed call.

A bodyguard?

If so, why hadn't he been here with him when he came to check out the abandoned facility?

A dealer then, one who was waiting on a fresh supply that he could give to his street-level distributors?

Or just a friend, one who was worried about him because he hadn't checked in.

A friend that knows where he is?

A chill arrived but then faded as he realized that if he had been concerned when coming out here, he would have brought others with him.

Still, he needed to know more about this Charles Fletcher.

Was he really some big-time drug dealer?

Nothing actually pointed to that being the case; he had just assumed it based on everything that Lyn had said. And she could not be trusted. Not after he had found out the truth about Billy.

Could this man have been sent by Billy?

Was Billy having people look for Lyn?

Had he accidentally killed one of the good guys?

If so, it would be forgiven.

Friendly-fire casualties happened in war, and this most certainly was a war. And not just any war, but The War. Nothing else in the history of mankind came close to the importance of this conflict. In fact, all the others were just simple blips on the screen when compared to it.

And you're spending the war sitting on your ass in an old commons room of a crumbling mental institution.

The thought caused him to pace.

Back and forth, from one corner to the next, his steps getting quicker and quicker as his frustration grew.

He had to do something.

He had to—

An idea arrived, one that he couldn't believe he hadn't considered earlier—especially when trying to figure out where the members of the Seven were located.

The wallet.

Inside was a driver's license.

And on the driver's license was an address.

All this time he had been asking himself questions about Charles Fletcher, theorizing on who exactly the man was, when all he had to do was go and see.

It was simple.

Maybe too simple...

Could it be a trap?

Had Satan sent this man here as a sacrifice simply to lure him away from the compound so that the Seven could then make a move?

The serpent was crafty and likely knew that he was growing weary of being holed up, given that he was a man of action. So the question was, did he continue to wait around for something to happen on the chance that it was some form of trickery, or did he go on the offensive?

Go on the offensive.

Spring the trap.

Plus, given that most of his supplies had been destroyed, he would need to make a move soon anyway.

He couldn't stay in the compound forever.

Hell, with a second mouth to feed, he couldn't stay there for more than a week.

He had no choice but to head out.

A new question arrived, this one concerning Lyn.

Did he leave her here or take her with him?

Both options were risky.

If he left her here, the Seven could swoop in and take her, but if he brought her with him, she might find a way to draw attention to him, which wouldn't be good.

Are they watching?

Are they waiting to make a move as soon as I leave?

During his patrols he hadn't been able to spot anyone surveilling the place, but if they were well trained and knew what they were doing, he could have been nearly on top of them during one of his passes and not seen them. Such had happened to him once while in Afghanistan. The enemy had gotten so close to him while heading out to relieve himself that he had nearly been pissed on.

A chance encounter that could have ruined the entire mission.

Something which one could not have foreseen or planned for.

Like the daughter showing up at Joel's house.

That had changed everything, had triggered a series of events that led straight to this moment.

What if she had not shown up?

Would he still have ended up here, trying to figure out what his next step would be?

Or would he and Lyn have crossed paths another way?

No.

This was the path the Lord had chosen, one that likely would have happened no matter what. In fact, if Joel's daughter hadn't shown up, maybe he still would have had to flee out this way, the police eventually finding something that pointed his way.

Or maybe he would have been out here adding more MREs to his supply cache when the three showed up, forcing him to confront them so that his fallback position would stay secure.

Would I have known about the girl and the Seven at that point?

Had it not been for the eclipse and the Father finally speaking to him, he would not have known what his mission was. And then, on top of that, had Lyn not called for help and revealed that the Seven were coming, he would not have realized she was the one he was supposed to be protecting.

Wait...

She called Billy.

Billy was not part of the Seven.

Oh...fuck.

For two days now he had been thinking she was the one he was supposed to be protecting simply because she had said seven people were coming to her rescue.

No, she hadn't even said seven. He had. She had simply nodded. While he was choking her.

What if he had said thirty?

Or ten?

Or sixteen?

Would she still have nodded so he would release her?

Or had the Lord guided things into a situation where she nodded so that he would realize she was the one and not kill her?

Which was it?

Why couldn't he have been given a name?

Why did everything have to be so vague?

Why—

Stop!

Trust in the Lord.

Everything was part of His plan.

Dwelling on what that plan was would get him nowhere. He simply needed to act. Instinct would guide him. And right now his instinct was telling him to go learn more about this Charles Fletcher person.

. . .

THE SUN WAS STILL in the sky when he left the compound, which normally would have been ill-advised given that darkness would better conceal his features, but he felt it was okay to take such a risk because locating a property during the daylight hours was easier than during the nighttime ones. And once he did that, he could then wait until darkness set in to make his move. Where exactly he would wait, he did not know, but wait he would, the area providing plenty of isolated riverside locations.

An hour later he was at one of those riverside locations, his eyes looking out at the water as the sun was setting behind him. Beer cans, fast-food wrappers, plastic bags, and spools of tangled-up fishing line mucked up the shoreline, marking the presence of mankind, but beyond it the water seemed perfect.

It isn't.

Within the water would be chemical pollutants from boat engines and factory runoffs.

Nothing was safe.

The history of humanity was one of mankind spoiling the beauty that God had created. From almost day one, mankind had been in conflict with the paradise God had provided.

Would that change?

Once the Lord reestablished His kingdom on Earth, would mankind finally live at peace with the rest of creation, or would everything simply repeat itself like it had after the great flood?

Josiah did not expect an answer and rather than sit around waiting for one, he pushed the question from his mind and shifted his attention to Charles Fletcher's phone.

Two calls had come in during the last hour, one from the Louis person, and one that was simply listed as Office.

The latter intrigued him because he wondered if that meant it was something to do with the drug trade.

Worry followed.

What if they were raiding the compound at that very moment?

What if—

Another call came in, though this one was on Lyn's phone.

He pulled it from his pocket as it finished ringing.

Billy.

He stared at this for several seconds and then nearly jumped when the phone buzzed again.

Voicemail.

Hesitation arrived, though he wasn't sure why.

Several seconds came and went.

The phone buzzed again.

This time it was a text.

He thumbed it open.

THINK ABOUT HER!

A picture was attached. One of a chubby round-face toddler in a colorful swimsuit dress standing on a riverside beach, a floppy hat protecting her face from the overhead sun.

Unease began to build.

Another text arrived.

What am I going to tell her when she starts asking about her mother?

Josiah simply stared.

Another text arrived.

And what if her father comes knocking on my door?

Josiah waited.

Do you really want that piece of shit getting custody by default?

Josiah wondered who the father was.

"Just some tweaker I fucked" would probably be her response, one that he knew he couldn't trust.

Everything she said seemed to be a lie, the only truth he had experienced thus far being the tears she had shed earlier when he had mentioned the get well soon card.

Were they real? he wondered. *Is she one of those women that can cry on command in order to get sympathy and better her situation?*

Another text arrived.

Look. I know it isn't your fault. The hospital fucked up and started you down this path with the painkillers. But you need to make the decision to get clean.

Josiah pondered that one for a moment, but then realized it likely had something to do with Lyn going to rehab.

And watching her kid?

Keeping her away from the father?

Protecting her?

Josiah turned around while thinking about this, his eyes checking the sun to see how close it was to the horizon.

The sun!

He thumbed open the phone and scrolled back through the texts until he came upon the picture of Lyn's daughter on the beach.

Clothed in the sun!

Was this the one the Father had been talking about?

Was he protecting the wrong one?

Was that why the Seven hadn't shown up at the compound?

Were they planning an attack on the daughter instead?

And if so, who was Charles Fletcher?

Was that the father?

Had he gone to the compound to find out where his daughter was?

Or had that simply been a random visit by someone who had nothing to do with this situation?

Indecision gripped him.

Why hadn't the Father given him a name?

One simple name and all of this would be very straight-forward.

"Protect so-and-so from the Seven."

Frustration appeared.

So much of the confusion with the world could be erased if the Lord would simply voice what was needed. If He were to appear in the sky and speak, humanity would listen.

Or would they?

He didn't really know.

And speculating upon all this was pointless.

He had a mission to fulfill, and while he didn't like some of the unknowns with the mission, he still needed to proceed.

His eyes glanced toward the sun once again.

Another hour.

He turned back to the water.

Time passed, slowly at first, but then seemed to speed up until his shadow stretched all the way to the other bank.

It was time.

Darkness had not yet arrived, but it would be in place by the time he got back to the house that Charles Fletcher lived in.

Would he find answers within?

Or just more questions?

Should I just go get Lyn's daughter instead?

EIGHTEEN

MEL'S PHONE began to ring while she was looking at Google Earth, her eyes uselessly scanning the various landscapes north of town to see what it was Dr. Fletcher might have been interested in checking out.

"Detective," she answered.

"Mel," Higgins replied. "I got your message."

"Obviously," she said.

He sighed.

"Dr. Fletcher is missing," she added.

"Not officially," he replied.

"Bullshit," she snapped. "He missed all his appointments today without notice."

Her phone buzzed.

She glanced at it.

It was a text from Nelson that read: *I'm in jail.*

Mel's eyes went wide.

"I take it Louis contacted you," Higgins said. It was not a question.

"Louis?" Mel asked, her mind stuck on the fact that Nelson was in jail. *Wait, how could he text from jail?*

"Charles's husband," Higgins said.

"What about him?"

A new text arrived. It read: *FB jail that is.*

Mel shook her head and then said, "What'd you say? Bad connection."

"I said, did Louis happen to mention that this isn't the first time Charles has done this?"

"Done what? Skipped out on his patients for a day without warning?"

"Disappeared for several hours while trying to find answers for a patient. He fancies himself an amateur detective, and then sometimes goes out and gets himself into trouble."

"Then you should go out and make sure he isn't in trouble," Mel snapped.

"Not that kind of trouble," Higgins said, voice suddenly exhausted.

"What do you mean?"

"Last time he did this, it was because he was trying to help a patient of his by proving that her husband was having an affair. He figured the relationship was toxic and that she needed to extract herself from it, and that learning the husband was cheating would finally push her in that direction. Meanwhile, the wife took some advice from a friend and tried to spice up their love life a bit. One thing led to another, and Charles ended up taking pictures of the two in the back seat of the husband's car while parked in an unofficial teenage lovers' lane along the river."

Mel let out a chuckle.

"It's not funny," Higgins scolded. "He nearly lost his job."

"Over some photos?" Mel asked.

"It was a pretty big deal."

"And what, because of that, you won't take him seriously even if maybe he learned his lesson and this time he actually has something legit that should be looked into?"

"That's just it, we did look into it. Even had a deputy go out to New—out there to check the place out. It was a bust."

"Out where?" Mel asked.

"Don't worry about it."

"I am worried. I think Dr. Fletcher is in trouble and so does Louis."

"He's fine. Trust me."

"I don't trust you."

Higgins didn't reply to that.

"Where did he go?" Mel demanded.

"It doesn't matter. Joseph Ellis didn't go there after the shooting."

"Then there is no reason not to tell me."

Higgins let out a brief laugh and then said, "No. The last thing I need is for you to go traipsing around that place and get hurt."

"What place?"

"Let it go."

"I need to know."

"Then ask Dr. Fletcher when he comes back."

Mel nearly threw her phone in frustration.

"Look," Higgins said. "I know you want answers. I would too if I had been through what you went through. But the best thing you can do right now is sit tight and let us do our job. That way we will get those answers for you."

"But you're not doing your job!"

"We are," he insisted.

"You think he went south and joined a militia group."

"All the evidence points toward—"

"That evidence is bullshit. He set a false trail, one that you all ate up hook, line, and sinker."

"Our analyst feels that is highly unlikely, given the situation and the one-track mindset that Joseph Ellis has displayed."

"Tell your analyst that he's a fucktard."

"She," Higgins said.

"Okay, *she's* a fucktard. *One-track mind.* Come on! This guy was a special forces soldier, one who was trained to get away from people like you."

"Yes, but that was before he was hit by an IED. Since then he could barely hold down a part-time janitorial job."

"IED?" Mel questioned.

"An Improvised Explosive Device," Higgins said. "It was the most common weapon used against soldiers in Iraq, which led to the Taliban using them in Afghanistan."

"That's not what happened."

"I have the official report right here. It clearly states that Master Sergeant Ellis was in a vehicle heading toward a suspected arms dump with several Afghan soldiers when an IED detonated beneath the vehicle. It killed two Afghan soldiers outright and severely wounded Sergeant Ellis."

"He was burned."

"I know. The IED caused the vehicle to catch fire after it was flipped over."

"No! He wasn't in a vehicle. He was lured into the back room of a house by a young woman who hit him in the face with a lantern."

Higgins went silent for several seconds, the sound of pages shuffling reaching her ears. "Did he tell you this?"

"What? No!"

"Then where did you hear it?"

Mel was a second away from mentioning Nelson but then stopped, an idea forming. "Hmm. You know. It seems we both have information the other wants. Maybe we should consider a trade."

"I'm not telling you where Dr. Fletcher went."

"Then I'm not telling you who I've been speaking with."

The two were at an impasse, one that was not resolved.

.   .   .

WHY ARE you in FB jail? Mel texted shortly after her conversation with Detective Higgins came to an end.

No reply was forthcoming, so she turned her attention back to the Google Earth map she had been looking at, her eyes once again uselessly scanning the area north of town to see if anything jumped out at her.

A text arrived.

Nelson.

It read: *I posted an opinion that some did not care for and it got reported as hate speech.*

Really? Mel texted back.

Yep.

Wow. So how long you in jail for?

A week.

A week!?

Yep. This isn't the first time I've clashed with the overly sensitive kumbaya crowd. They just don't seem to realize the world is a nasty place.

Downstairs, the front door opened, her mother calling out to her.

Mel ignored it.

So, any word from your doctor? he asked.

No, Mel typed but then hesitated before hitting Send.

Nelson waited, likely staring at a dot bubble beneath his text bubble.

But I spoke to his husband, who said he was heading somewhere north of here, she added and hit Send.

His husband?

You have a problem with that?

No. Of course not. Where does he think he went?

He didn't say and the police won't tell me, but I know it was north of here.

What's north of here?

I don't know.

But the police do?

Yeah.

Did they check it out?

They claim they did, but it was probably half-assed.

"Mel?" her mother called up the stairs. "I got chicken."

Mel twisted toward her door while thinking, *Chicken?*

Lately they had each been fending for themselves during mealtimes, her mother eating weird diet shit while Mel hit up one of the fast-food joints near the highway. Tonight she had been thinking Chipotle. But if her mother had gotten them a bucket of chicken...

We should go talk to his husband, see if we can get any more info, Nelson said.

He doesn't know where he went, just that it was north of here, Mel reminded him.

What other options do we have? We're not exactly closing in on him.

Mel hesitated.

Plus, he might know more than he realizes, especially if Dr. Fletcher had notes.

A dot bubble appeared below that.

Mel waited.

And just think, if you find out where Dr. Fletcher went and then actually help save his life, you'll be a hero.

Mel liked the idea of being considered a hero. Especially once school started, the wide-eyed looks, glares, and muffled voices she had heard while picking up her books the other day having given her a good idea of just how horrible the first few weeks and even months of her junior year were going to be.

"Mel?" her mother called again.

"Coming!" Mel shouted and then looked down at her phone.

Indecision paralyzed her.

She headed downstairs to grab a piece of chicken while she considered this.

A KFC bucket was on the table, along with several different side items and two plate settings.

A pamphlet was present as well, one that sat atop her plate.

What the...? her mind started as her eyes took in the display of young women wearing dull uniforms standing outside a building that had a tower that looked almost medieval.

A school for girls?

Recognition arrived.

She can't be thinking—

Her mom came into the room, a glass of something that was likely wine in her hand.

"What's this?" Mel asked, holding up the pamphlet.

"It's where I went to school," her mother said, an odd smile on her face.

"Yeah, I know that! Why are you showing me this?"

"Because I feel it is time we made some changes, ones that will provide a better direction for you." She sipped her wine.

"A better direction?"

"Yes. One that will help you focus on your future." She took another sip. "And I spoke to the headmistress today, and while it is a bit late for enrollment, she agreed that given the circumstances, they can pull some strings to get you into classes and one of the dorms by the end of next week."

"Dorms?"

"Well, it is in New England, so you can't exactly take a bus every day."

"What the fuck?" Mel demanded. "You can't just ship me off to New England!"

"I can and will if I think it is for the best." Another sip. "Oh, and they are a bit old-fashioned when it comes to discipline, and I plan on signing a waiver, so you might want to try cleaning up your language."

Mel was at a complete loss for words.

And then something clicked.

"You're just trying to scare me," she said, grabbing a piece of chicken. "There is no way you can afford this."

"Actually..." she said and let her words fade.

"Actually what?" Mel asked, horror appearing.

"You know all those calls I made that you ignored today."

Mel didn't reply to that.

"I was trying to let you know that your father's life-insurance policy has been approved."

Oh, no, no, no, no, no!

"And it will more than cover the costs for you to finish up school out there."

Once again, Mel was at a loss for words.

"We leave on Monday."

"I'm not going," Mel said, dropping her chicken, appetite gone.

"You don't have a choice in this."

"I do have a choice, and I'm making it." She picked up the pamphlet and began tearing it into pieces, grease from the chicken smearing across the images.

Her mother simply smiled, which was worse than any vocal reply.

Mel was fucked.

So much so that she wanted to cry, the tears starting to fall as she made her way back into her room.

She couldn't take it anymore.

One thing led to another.

And with this latest development, it was almost like her mother was using her father's death to strike a final blow.

It was too much.

He would not have wanted this.

The money from a life-insurance policy was supposed to help a family in need after one died, not be used to ship a daughter off to a boarding school so that the mother could have the house to herself.

Shit, why was her mother even the one receiving the money?

After two years of being divorced, her father should have changed the recipient.

Who would he have changed it to?

Me?

I totally fucked him over during the divorce.

And now she has all the money.

But why would she spend it on me?

She wouldn't have put it all toward the school if that's all there was.

No way.

The policy must have been quite substantial.

A text arrived.

It was Nelson.

He was still waiting for an answer.

NINETEEN

THE SINGLE-STORY RANCH house was occupied. This was obvious given that lights were on within and figures could be seen moving about. How many figures, Josiah didn't know. Three for sure. Two in the front room while a third was in the far room at the end. If there were others, they were beyond his current line of sight.

The light went off in the far room, the figure from that room joining the others in the front room.

Josiah waited and watched.

No one else appeared.

Three it was.

What exactly they were doing, he didn't know, but it seemed like a meeting of some sort given that the three seemed to be grouped together as if having a discussion. Two on one side, the one from the room at the end on the other.

Planning an attack on the compound?

Or an attack on the little girl in the picture?

Or neither?

Could this be a completely harmless get-together, one that didn't concern him at all?

No.

This was important.

How so, he didn't know, but he felt that once he was inside and facing those three, answers would arrive.

And not just any answers.

Important ones.

Answers that might finally give him a path forward.

But first he had to get inside and subdue the three, all without the authorities being alerted.

Or their own backup.

If they were part of the Seven.

This would be tricky.

Had it been a kill mission, he wouldn't have a problem. In and out. But this...it was more like a snatch-and-grab, though without the snatching and grabbing since he would most likely keep them here and do the interrogation in the main room.

These were always the toughest, the ones that had produced the most groans when in Afghanistan.

Blue eyes.

Soft skin.

Bare breasts.

Tears.

Screams.

No! No! No!

He punched the steering wheel to try to stop the memories before the burning sensation arrived, pain from his broken finger exploding just as the horn echoed in the quiet neighborhood.

It worked.

He took a deep breath.

Worry followed.

Had anyone heard the horn?

That had been a mistake, one that he couldn't afford right now.

No one seemed interested in the car, the three figures in the main room still gathered around whatever they were looking at, all while the rest of the neighborhood was quiet.

The only exception to this was a figure about a block ahead walking a dog.

Could they be a lookout?

If so, they were a bit obvious about it, which made him think they were not a lookout.

Then again, the obviousness of their disguise might be purposeful, one that was designed to throw someone like him off.

Take them out?

No.

The dog was their safety net.

If the dog didn't alert them to his approach prior to his killing stroke, it certainly would alert others afterward by barking, and trying to take out a dog along with a person while on a neighborhood street would be too problematic.

He would leave them alone.

A few seconds later, the figure and the dog vanished around a corner up ahead.

He turned his attention back to the house.

The three were still in the front room, though now one of them was standing. Why exactly he didn't know, but standing they were, arms moving about as if something heated were being discussed.

A disagreement about how to proceed?

Strife among the Seven?

If so, this was the perfect time for him to strike.

THE BACKYARD WAS WELL KEPT and secluded from the neighbors, given the privacy fence and the vegetation that had been planted along it. No lock was on the gate to the fence, which meant one of two things. Either someone had gotten careless as the sun set, or the sole purpose of the fence and vegetation was to keep the neighbors from seeing into the yard.

Whichever it was, it currently worked to his advantage since no one could see him as he approached the back porch, which had been roofed over and nicely styled with brick half-walls, a cozy seating area, and a really nice BBQ setup.

French-style doors led into the house, doors that were not locked.

A trap?

Or was God's hand helping him by making those inside careless when it came to locks?

Either way, he crossed the threshold of the house.

Voices echoed from the front room, which sat just beyond the kitchen, light spilling in from the doorway cutout.

One was female.

Why this caught him off guard, he did not know, but it did.

Could one of the Seven actually be a woman?

Why not?

Satan had been using women since the very beginning, Eve being the sole reason humanity had been kicked out of paradise and burdened with sin.

"*And this is why you must purify yourself,*" the Father had often said. "*Satan uses women to corrupt men, especially those chosen by God.*"

Samson was a perfect example of this.

Had it not been for his being seduced by a woman, his hair would not have been sheared.

Others had suffered as well, always because they had let their lust for women get the better of them.

Not him though.

He had come close on several occasions, but had been able to resist the urges.

But would he be able to continue to resist?

"If you don't purify yourself, you will fail."

"Sure, help yourself," a voice said, bringing him back to the present.

Steps echoed as someone came toward the kitchen.

Josiah quickly ducked into a side room that had a washer and dryer along a wall, his breathing slowing while his hand pulled his pistol free.

The sound of bottles rattling as the fridge was opened reached his ears.

Drink selected, the fridge was closed and the figure headed back into the front room.

Joseph took a silent breath and stepped out of the side room.

"Changed your mind?" a voice asked.

"Yep," the female replied just as she stepped through the cutout and into the kitchen.

She stopped, eyes going wide as she saw him.

Surprise hit.

Joel's daughter.

What was she—?

A gasp and then a shout cut off his thought, his body springing into action as she took a step back while twisting, ready to flee.

MEL DIDN'T BELIEVE her eyes. Couldn't believe them. It wasn't possible. *He* couldn't be here. Not in Louis's kitchen.

She blinked.

He was still there.

It was real.

Run!

She tried, but he was quick for his size and hit her back with a force that felt like a wrecking ball, her body losing its balance as she toppled forward, head missing the coffee table by mere inches.

A gasp and then a grunt echoed.

Mel twisted just in time to see Nelson falling to the ground, one hand on his face where he had likely been pistol-whipped, blood visible between his fingers.

"On the ground," Joseph said, voice oddly calm.

Louis did as instructed, his hands up in the air.

"Facedown," Joseph added.

Louis complied.

And then the gun was pointing at her.

Mel stared at it.

"You're part of the Seven," Joseph said.

Mel didn't know how to reply to that.

"Answer me!" he demanded.

"I-I-" she started, unsure what he was talking about, her eyes watching as Nelson sprang up and hit the arm that held the gun, knocking it loose.

"You!" Joseph cried.

"Me!" Nelson replied and then grunted as his body was slammed into the wall.

Gun!

Get it!

Mel sprang up from the floor and hurried toward it, her fingers hooking it by the trigger guard.

Another grunt echoed as Nelson's body was slammed into the wall for a second time.

"Stop!" Louis cried as he grabbed Joseph from behind.

Mel hadn't even seen him get up, but he had and now was trying to headlock the giant.

He failed, an elbow to the gut ending his attack.

Mel pointed the gun just as Nelson stuck a thumb into Joseph's left eye.

A horrible scream filled the room.

"Freeze!" Mel shouted, pointing the gun.

Joseph didn't freeze, mostly because Nelson was on him again, his attempt at a headlock far better than Louis's had been, though equally ineffective, Joseph simply grabbing his arm, flipping him up and over his own body.

Nelson hit the ground hard.

Mel fired.

JOSIAH HEARD the gunshot but didn't react to it, his focus squarely on Nelson, his initial surprise at seeing the man quickly replaced by anger and then hatred, the latter so intense that nothing else mattered.

Nelson twisted while on the floor, kicking at his knee.

Josiah jerked away from the blow and then reached for Nelson's leg, missed, and then grabbed the other as he tried to get up, the fall that followed one that was so awkward, it gave him pause.

Nelson started to pull himself away, all while Josiah yanked him back, an odd snap echoing, along with another gunshot.

Josiah hit the wall, Nelson's leg in his hands.

It wasn't real.

He stared in dismay for a few seconds and then jerked as a bullet ricocheted off one of the metal hinges, striking him in the hip.

It felt like a bee sting.

Nelson was getting away.

Josiah charged, a memory of grabbing him off the teenage Afghan girl and throwing him across the room echoing within his mind.

Someone had then grabbed him from the side.

Josiah broke that man's arm and then hit the third member

of Nelson's team, the blow to his face knocking all sense from him as he crumpled onto the dirt floor.

A gunshot echoed, both in his memory and reality.

Back then it had been Nelson shooting at him with a pistol; this time it was Joel's daughter.

Neither one hit him.

Josiah brought the leg down, crushing Nelson's left arm as he tried to block the blow, a crunch echoing.

Nelson shifted as the second blow came down, this one missing his head and shattering his shoulder instead.

The third blow crushed his face.

Fire!

It engulfed him as the Afghan girl smashed an oil lamp against his head, the flames leaping all over him.

More gunshots echoed, his mind unable to make out who was shooting who, the only thing that mattered being the flames and his attempt at getting away from them.

Someone grabbed him.

He hit them with the leg, the sound of it shattering bringing him from his memory and back into the present.

Only the flames didn't disappear.

His flesh was burning.

He ran.

Right through the glass of the French-styled doors.

Another gunshot echoed, this one catching part of his clothing.

He didn't stop.

He couldn't stop.

This mission had been a failure.

Now all he could do was get away so that he could live to fight another day.

MEL GAVE chase without even thinking about it, her finger squeezing the trigger several times as she ran.

And then he was in a car, speeding away.

She tried to shoot out the tires, but missed with every shot.

"Drop it!" a voice commanded.

Mel blinked and then looked to her right.

A man was standing in a driveway, a rifle pointed at her.

She stared at him for several seconds before letting the pistol fall from her fingers.

Sirens echoed.

She turned.

"Stop!" the man demanded.

"Fuck off," Mel snapped back and headed back into the house.

TWENTY

"THE SOONER YOU explain what happened, the sooner you get to go home," Detective Simmons said.

Mel looked at him and said, "Maybe I don't want to go home."

Simmons sighed and leaned back in his chair.

"Tell us more about the young man you were with," Higgins said, his own body leaning forward.

"I've told you everything I know about him."

"Half of which isn't true."

"Says you."

"Says the military."

Mel shook her head. "He told me he was a part of Joseph Ellis's team in Afghanistan."

"And you believed him?"

"Why would he lie about that?"

"To get attention. People love pretending to be veterans."

"He was missing a leg."

"Lots of people are missing legs. Not all of them are veterans."

"Joseph knew him."

"Now see, that's where things get interesting," Higgins said. "Here he told you they were army buddies and that Joseph saved his life at one point, yet the moment they see each other, Joseph tries to kill him by beating him to death with his own leg."

Simmons snorted.

Higgins gave him a look.

Simmons waved a hand.

"You think it's funny?" Mel asked, her mind trying to shake away the memory of seeing the leg hitting Nelson's face.

"I think it's fucking hilarious," Simmons said.

Mel lunged across the table, fists swinging.

"Whoa, whoa!" Higgins cried, grabbing her.

"Were you two shacking up?" Simmons asked, amusement present. "Is that why they tried to kill each other? A bit of jealousy maybe?"

"Fuck you!" Mel snarled, her arms trying to wrestle free of Higgins's grip.

"Easy!" Higgins snapped.

"Touchy subject, it seems," Simmons said, voice calm. "What exactly do you have going on with these two?"

"Nothing!" Mel spat.

"Then why are they both fixated on you?"

"I don't know!"

A knock echoed.

Simmons went to the door and stepped out while Higgins nudged her back to her chair. "You cool?"

"Fuck you," Mel said and then took a seat.

"Dean," Simmons said.

Higgins turned and looked at him and then stepped out into the hall as well.

Mel waited.

Seconds turned to minutes, her eyes wandering around the room, concern that her fear might be evident getting the better of her. She wanted to remain stoic in their presence, wanted to show that she didn't give a shit about all this, but couldn't. It was all too much.

It was...

The door opened.

Higgins stepped back in, a startled look on his face. "Dr. Fletcher is dead."

"Dead?"

Higgins nodded.

Mel didn't know how to reply.

"They found his body in the trunk of a car up at New Eden," he added.

"New Eden?" Mel asked, the name familiar, but unplaceable.

"It's an old mental institution an hour north of here," Higgins said. "Charles was convinced that Joseph Ellis had gone up there to hide out."

"Why?"

"The straitjacket."

"The one I was in?" she asked and then mentally kicked herself with a "duh."

Higgins nodded while taking a seat, his body sort of oozing into the chair, almost as if he were struggling to stay on his feet.

Guilt? Mel wondered.

"He tracked the make of it down to an old supplier back in the fifties that had sent a shipment to New Eden."

"And you refused to check it out?" Mel asked, anger replacing her sadness.

"We had the county take a look at the place to see if he was up there. They checked it out and said it was empty."

"And yet it wasn't." She crossed her arms.

He didn't reply to that.

"How does it feel to know you're responsible for his death?" she asked.

That stung. She could see it in his eyes. Yet he didn't lash out. In fact, he didn't say anything to defend himself. Instead, he asked, "Did Joseph say anything at all during tonight's incident?"

"Incident? You're calling this an incident?"

"Just answer the question."

"No, he didn't say—" She stopped, a memory surfacing, one that finally replaced the image of Nelson being beaten with his own leg.

Higgins saw the look and waited.

"He said something about the number seven."

"Seven?"

"Yeah."

"Did he say anything like that before, while you were in his grandmother's house?"

She thought about this for several seconds and then shook her head.

"You're sure?"

"Yeah. I would have remembered something like that."

"Seven," he repeated.

She waited, the fingers on her right hand picking at the small bandage on her left. Beneath the bandage was a tiny burn, one that she hadn't noticed until the police handcuffed her.

Another knock echoed.

"Busy night," Higgins muttered and went to the door.

Once again, she was alone.

She waited.

And waited.

And waited.

Something had happened, something bigger than them finding Dr. Fletcher's body. But what?

She got up and cautiously went to the door.

Locked.

Fuckers!

After the detectives had arrived and removed the handcuffs, she had assumed that meant she was not under arrest, but now—

The door opened.

She backed up, an odd sense of feeling like she had been caught doing something she shouldn't arriving.

"Your mother is here and going to take you home," Higgins said, voice rushed. "A squad car will be outside your place tonight to keep an eye on things."

"What happened?" she asked as he tried to usher her from the room.

"Nothing you need to worry about," he said, hand on her back.

She twisted away, crossed her arms, and glared at him. "Tell me."

"They found someone at New Eden," he said after a moment of hesitation. "While going room to room. He's in pretty bad shape—"

Footsteps echoed as Simmons hurried toward him. "They just found another, but this one didn't make it."

"Shit."

Simmons looked at Mel, eyes narrowing. "What's going on?"

"I'm sending her home," Higgins said.

Simmons didn't react to this and instead said, "I'll meet you at the car."

"Roger that," Higgins said and then motioned for Mel to keep moving.

"VISIT WHO?" her mother asked. Then, before Mel could even answer, "Is this the thirty-five-year-old guy you've been seeing?"

"Seeing? I've haven't been 'seeing' anyone. He's a soldier that served in Afghanistan with Joseph Ellis who wanted to try and see if he could help."

"From what the police told me, he is not a soldier and he has simply been scamming you."

"The police don't know what they're talking about," Mel said, though she herself now had some doubts about Nelson. "He simply wants to help, and if it weren't for him, I would probably be dead right now."

"If it weren't for him, you wouldn't have gone out at all and wouldn't have needed his protection."

Mel sighed and turned toward the passenger window.

"I don't want you leaving the house until we head out on Monday," her mother said.

"Whatever," Mel muttered.

"I'm serious."

Mel didn't reply.

Nothing else was said until they arrived back home, Mel silently noting the squad car that was parked in front of the house.

"Honey, we'll get through this," her mother said while pulling into the garage.

"We?" Mel demanded. "*We?* I'm sorry, were you the one who was kept in a straitjacket for two weeks after being attacked by a naked man? Were you the one who had to kill an old lady because she was trying to clobber you with a rolling pin? Were you the one who had to run to the police while nearly naked and covered in her own piss? Were you the one who has had to face countless accusations from people all across the planet who feel you were the one that instigated the entire thing? Were you—"

"You're not the only one who has—"

"Don't you dare compare what you have gone through with what I went through!" Mel shouted and stepped out of the car, only to shout again as she turned and came face-to-face with a young police officer.

"Sorry, ma'am, didn't mean to startle you," the young officer said while removing his hat. "I just wanted to introduce myself since I'll be—"

"Fuck off," Mel snapped and headed inside, hearing her mother apologizing to the officer on her behalf.

Her computer awaited, her fingers quickly bringing it back to life with a nudge of the mouse and a password that her mother would never be able to guess.

Facebook was still up, the messages she and Louis had been sharing about getting together to look through Dr. Fletcher's files to see if they could figure out where he went still on display.

Had Nelson been right?

Had Joseph Ellis been following her?

Is that why he had shown up there?

Or had he simply headed there to see what had led Dr. Fletcher to his hideout, his hope being to eliminate the evidence so others wouldn't follow?

Others had found him though.

Two at least, one who was dead.

What had he done to them?

And why?

New Eden.

She typed it into Google.

Over thirty million results were returned, none of which looked very promising as she scrolled down the first page.

Next she tried *New Eden Mental Hospital.*

These results looked more promising. In fact, the very first one reminded her of why the name had pinged something within her mind. It was an old news story about a kid that had gone missing, one whose body had been found trapped inside a self-locking room at the old New Eden Mental Hospital back in 2008. Lawsuits had followed as the parents tried to sue everyone they could over the death. Mel didn't read enough of the article to find out if the lawsuits had been successful. One thing she did know, public opinion had not been on their side back then, many wondering why a ten-year-old had been allowed to wander around an abandoned mental institution on his own ten miles from town. Something was fishy about that, some going so far as to theorize that the parents had actually locked him in the room themselves in order to kill him and then try to collect on the death.

Mel had no opinion one way or the other.

All she cared about now was figuring out what Joseph Ellis had been doing at the mental institution and how it played into her father's death.

Does it play into it at all?

Was it just a place he knew about and decided to hide out in after the shooting?

No.

Joseph Ellis had obviously been interested in the place before the attack on her father, given that he had brought items like the straitjacket to his grandmother's place.

But why?

What had he been planning?

NELSON.

Josiah had never once considered the man when contemplating the identities of the Seven, yet now that his involvement had been revealed, it all made perfect sense. After all, who better to lead the Seven against him than the one who was responsible for his disfigurement?

Of course, this now meant that the list of names he had from Alec was suspect.

Had the young man lied to him?

Had he simply said yes to certain names in hopes that it would keep him from being hurt?

Why would someone do that?

Once the lie was uncovered, pain would follow, pain that would be far worse than anything that would have been done in an attempt to extract the names the first time around.

That's what drug addicts do, a voice said, one that sounded similar to the Father's. *They live in the moment, consequences be damned.*

Tweakers, Josiah muttered to himself.

That was what Lyn would have called them.

She was one herself, one that had wasted his time.

Or had she?

Without her coming to the compound, he never would have realized it was her daughter that he was supposed to find and protect.

One thing had led to another.

Like dominoes.

And Nelson had tipped the first one over back in Afghanistan.

Or had he?

If Josiah had not joined the military, he would never have met Nelson.

It went further back.

His entire life was a string of dominoes, the first one too far back for him to recall.

Focus.

Protect her from the Seven.

Wounding Nelson had been a good first step, but given what the man had already recovered from, he knew it would only be temporary. Nelson needed to be eliminated.

One more strike with the leg would have done it.

Josiah had no doubt about this, and had it not been for Joel's daughter, he would have been successful.

Joel's daughter.

Everything was coming back around, the domino string looping itself.

It was surreal.

Yet it also made sense.

Nelson had always been good at recruiting locals to help in his missions. It was one of the reasons why his private military company had been able to undercut other private military companies in Afghanistan.

His boss would give Nelson information on a snatch-and-grab, and he would go out and find indigenous personnel that could help in securing the target.

And now that was what he was doing here.

Joel's daughter, the tweakers, Charles Fletcher...Nelson had likely recruited them all, their mission being twofold: kill him and secure Lyn's daughter.

But why?

Who had hired him?

Had he been hired?

Or was he acting on his own?

If the former, it meant there were monied institutions involved, ones that could afford the costs of having someone like Nelson out in the field for several days.

A few years ago, Josiah would have scoffed at such a suggestion, but now, given what he had seen and experienced, he knew that Satan's minions could have easily worked their way to the top of many powerful companies and organizations, both in the private and public sector. Everything was contaminated, everything suspect.

How far back does it go?

Had Nelson been raping that blue-eyed girl in Afghanistan as a lure?

Did I walk into a trap?

Josiah shuddered at the thought, the idea that he had had a

target on him for so long without even being aware unsettling.

Yet he had survived.

Nelson had powerful men behind him, ones with money and influence, but they were no match for one who had God on his side.

Josiah's continued existence was evidence of this.

Nelson had failed in his attempts at eliminating him.

Twice.

That did not bode well for him.

His employer would be displeased.

Of this, Josiah had no doubt.

But they would likely give him another chance, which was worrisome because that would be an attempt that Nelson could not fail. Equally worrisome would be the desperation that would now be a driving force for the enemy. What type of actions would they take to achieve their desired results? Would caution be dismissed? Would they simply go after their objective without worry of being discovered? Was stealth and secrecy no longer an important factor in their actions?

These thoughts plagued him as he crouched within the bushes along the fence in the backyard of the house, his eyes watching for a pattern in the patrols that the young officer made as he tried to keep Joel's daughter and the residence secure.

Josiah wanted to act. Needed to act. But he waited. Patience and discipline would win this particular fight. And he had time. This evening's events would have caused disorder within the enemy's ranks. It would take them a while to get reorganized. And with Nelson temporarily out of commission, they would have to rely on someone who would have been a second choice when considering their champion, which would put them at a disadvantage. After all, if someone like Nelson couldn't take him down, how would a second-stringer accomplish it?

TWENTY-ONE

MEL OPENED HER EYES.

Something was wrong.

She didn't know what, but the feeling was too strong to deny.

3:22 a.m.

She hadn't been asleep long.

Less than an hour.

He's here!

In the house!

She slipped free of the bedsheets, body ready to spring into action, all while her mind tried to process everything.

Nothing.

The house was quiet.

Too quiet, her mind suggested, but then dismissed the thought. At this time of night, it would always be quiet.

Still, something had jolted her awake, something that was not a normal sound within the house.

Had it even been a sound?

No answer followed.

She had no idea what it was that had awakened her, but knew something had and that it had triggered a warning.

MEL WAS HALFWAY DOWN the stairs when she heard the unmistakable sound of a boot on tile, one that had been lowered to the floor quietly in an attempt to go unnoticed as the intruder crept through the kitchen toward the front hallway.

Pepper spray in hand, she waited and listened, concern that her own steps would be heard if she continued down the stairs toward the landing.

Hinges groaned as a door was opened, and then the sudden but brief roar of an overhead fan as the light switch in the hallway bathroom was turned on and then off.

Mel used that moment to finish her descent, one step letting out a brief groan that likely seemed louder to her than it actually was.

No reaction.

She rounded the banister and started down the front hallway, her steps completely muffled by the thick, fuzzy socks she was wearing.

Up ahead the dark kitchen loomed, the back sliding porch door likely the point of entry.

Two doors were present to her left, one leading to the cellar, the other the bathroom that the intruder had peeked into.

But where had he gone from there?

Why not continue down the hallway toward the stairs?

Unless...

Pepper spray ready, she took hold of the knob on the bathroom door and threw it open, her eyes expecting to see the scarred giant inside, waiting for her to pass on by so he could take her from behind.

Instead, she saw the police officer, his pants around his ankles as he sat on the toilet, surprise and then pain echoing as a burst of pepper spray caught him square in the face.

"Oh God!" Mel shouted as he fell from the toilet, hands clutching his face, her own steps halted by the sudden burning in her eyes and sinuses.

She backed up and hit the wall.

"*Mel!*"

"*Mom!*" she tried to reply, her voice halted as fluids ran down her throat.

She blindly wobbled toward the kitchen, one hand outstretched along the wall while the other kept rubbing at her eyes.

"*Mel, what happened?*"

Mel did not reply as she found the sink and turned on the faucet.

"*Are you okay?*"

The cold water felt good against her face, but seemed to do little in ridding herself of the irritation.

"*Mel!*"

She continued splashing water.

"*Mel!*" her mother screamed again.

An explosion followed, one that caused Mel to drop down behind the counter, right into a pool of water she had created.

Another explosion, followed by the sound of glass breaking.

A screamed echoed.

It sounded like her mother.

Mel blinked several times and rubbed her eyes.

Another scream, this one filled with fury.

Two more explosions, ones that Mel finally realized were gunshots.

She peeked around the corner of the kitchen island.

The glass in the sliding door had been shot out.

Another gunshot, this one right over her head.

She ducked back behind the counter, ears ringing.

JOSIAH HAD PLANNED on taking out the officer as he patrolled through the backyard, his body positioned perfectly on the far side of the porch, a row of overgrown bushes concealing him.

But then the officer did something he wasn't expecting, something he hadn't done on previous patrols. He went into the house. Right through the back door, which was apparently unlocked.

Surprise appeared, followed by concern.

A trap?

Were they trying to lure him inside where dozens of officers were waiting?

Had this entire night been one big trap?

No.

The events at Charles Fletcher's house had not been a trap.

But this...

Abort?

Go secure Lyn's daughter instead?

Indecision hung heavy.

He didn't know what to do.

Protect her from the Seven.

Joel's daughter was part of the Seven.

Or was she?

Every time he thought he knew who they were and who he was supposed to be protecting, things got all jumbled up.

It just wasn't right.

How was he supposed to carry out his mission when his objective was so poorly conveyed to him?

Could this be why the enemy had done so well in recent years?

Did they communicate more clearly with those who had agreed to do their bidding?

Or was his lack of commitment to blame?

The Father had insisted that in order to succeed he needed to purify himself fully, his bony fingers confirming that such purification had not been performed one night while the two were talking.

Josiah still remembered the horrifying moment.

The Father had gone from being barely audible as he struggled to communicate, to shouting with a fury that had never been displayed before, his voice escaping from the room and echoing down the sterile hallways, alerting staff members who had hurried to the room, their eyes startled to see Josiah trying to remove the Father's fingers from his penis.

Things had changed after that.

Joel had put an end to the sessions and made it clear that Josiah was not to visit with the Father from that point forward, all while his own boss had given him a new area of the compound to focus on during the nights he was on duty.

It had been a humiliating blow, yet one that had been necessary given that it had set things in motion.

If I fail again...

He let the thought fade as bullets flew overhead, the ex-wife doing her own version of "spray and pray" with the pistol that she had carried downstairs.

Meanwhile, the daughter was on the opposite side of the island counter that he had positioned himself behind after stepping through the back door to see what all the screaming was about, the gunshots having caught him off guard.

He waited.

The gunshots stopped.

A quick peek around the corner revealed the ex-wife

trying to reload, her fingers fumbling with the pistol until the magazine fell free and hit the tile floor.

He took aim, his own pistol perfectly positioned for a center-mass shot.

Something crashed into his back just as he pulled the trigger, his aim jolted.

He fired several more times, all while the daughter tried to strangle him, her arms having found his throat and encircled it after pouncing on him like an angry cat.

The gun emptied.

He dropped it while standing, the girl's weight barely registering as he got to his feet and twisted himself so that he could slam her into the edge of the counter.

She grunted with the blow but would not let go.

He slammed her again, this time much harder than before.

One of her hands released, her body sagging as she lost her grip.

And then the other let go.

He twisted to face her, his hands reaching up to grab her by the throat.

She grinned.

An icy chill slithered through his bowels, one that quickly warmed as she withdrew the kitchen knife.

His fingers released her throat and reached down for the wound, his legs stumbling him backward, straight into a table that filled a breakfast nook.

Blood oozed.

Pain erupted.

It was unlike anything he had ever felt before.

And then his legs disappeared, the world twisting sideways as he fell, his skull bouncing once as it hit the floor.

MEL'S back was on fire as she stood over Joseph Ellis, knife in hand, blood dripping from the blade.

"Why'd you kill my father?" she asked, voice struggling to control the rage she felt.

He didn't reply, his eyes simply blinking, pain evident on his face.

"Mel, stay back," her mother cautioned as she approached, her hands shaking as she pointed the gun at the scarred giant.

Blood was running down her leg from a wound in her hip.

"Mom," Mel said. "You're shot!"

"What?" her mother questioned and looked down, face going pale.

"Mom!" Mel cried, free hand reaching toward her as her mother started to wobble.

The gun fell from her fingers.

Joseph grabbed it before Mel could even make a move toward it, the barrel quickly pointing her way, her eyes unable to focus on anything but the tiny circle of darkness that was about to erupt.

JOSIAH AIMED the gun at the daughter's face and pulled the trigger.

Nothing.

He tried again, but it wouldn't work.

MEL WAITED for the bullet to hit her in the face, but nothing happened.

She blinked.

Joseph seemed equally surprised.

Move!

She obeyed, her hand slashing out with the knife, razor

edge catching the wrist that held the gun, skin parting and blood flowing.

Once again, the gun fell.

Mel put a foot atop it and slid it away from Joseph Ellis and then stabbed down with the knife, his body twisting at the last second, the point going into his side rather than his chest, a horrible blade-on-bone screech racing along her nerves as her fingers slid down the edge upon its sudden stop.

"Get back," a wary voice said, a new gun in her line of sight.

It was the officer from the bathroom.

Mel cradled her wounded fingers against her stomach as he guided her back toward the kitchen island.

Joseph pulled the knife free and dropped it, blood erupting from the new wound, his lips mumbling something that Mel could not understand.

Sirens echoed in the distance.

The officer got on the radio and reported the situation.

JOSIAH HAD FAILED.

He recognized this as he lay bleeding on the floor, his body unable to crawl away. It wasn't the wounds that stopped him, though they certainly were agonizing, but the gun that the officer held on him, one that was quickly joined by others as police flooded the house.

Medical personnel arrived as well, ones who triggered flashbacks to the airlift that had arrived after he had been burned.

No helicopter was present this time around.

Instead, it was just an ambulance with paramedics, ones who needed a few extra hands in loading him up into the vehicle, a police officer joining them in the back as they headed to whatever hospital they were taking him to, a handcuff linking his left wrist to the gurney.

Words were spoken among the chaos.

At first, he didn't understand them, but then realized they were asking him if he knew his name.

"Josiah," he said.

"Josiah?" the medic asked.

Josiah nodded.

More questions followed, but he couldn't focus on the words, his mind growing more and more hazy.

The girl?

Was she okay?

Someone was shaking his hand, lightly.

It was an officer, one in combat fatigues rather than a dress uniform.

"Don't worry, son, we took care of them," the officer said. "They fucked with the wrong team."

No, Josiah groaned.

Something jolted him.

The officer was gone.

In his place was a paramedic who was struggling to get him lowered from the ambulance, the blood-red lights of a sign that he could not read overhead.

"Jesus, a little help!" the paramedic cried.

Others came to his aid, the gurney finally lowered onto the pavement and wheeled into the hospital, a team seemingly ready for him, words like "bowel puncture" and "blood pressure" and "shooting suspect" echoing all around him.

NO ONE HANDCUFFED her this time. In fact, no one really paid much attention to her as she sat off in the corner of the kitchen, a dish towel wrapped around her fingers, the police's and paramedics' only focus being her mother and Joseph Ellis.

At one point the officer that she had pepper-sprayed in the bathroom did come over to her and asked if she was okay. She mumbled something back that wasn't even intelligible to her own ears, but must have registered as a yes to him.

"You know, you saved my life," he said.

She blinked and then asked, "How?"

"Well, I'm guessing he was out there on the porch waiting for me to step back out, but instead he ended up coming inside to find out what all the shouting was about after you sprayed me in the face, so..." He held up his hands. "Thanks."

"No problem," she said. And then, "How'd you get in?"

"Your mom gave me the key just in case I needed to use the bathroom," he said.

Mel didn't reply to that.

For a moment, it looked as if he was going to say something more, but then someone called his name and he hurried over to him.

Gave him the key, Mel said to herself and shook her head, an odd desire to chuckle arriving.

"You okay?" someone asked, her laughter catching him off guard.

"Yeah," she said, wiping at her face.

A look of horror crossed the man's face. "Are you bleeding?" he asked.

"I was, but I think it—" She looked at the dishtowel, which had become soaked with blood. "Uh-oh," was all she managed after that, the room suddenly spinning.

Arms caught her before she toppled over, a call for help echoing within her mind as everything started to fade.

PART FOUR
THE HOSPITAL

TWENTY-TWO

"TWICE IN ONE NIGHT," Detective Higgins said, setting a cup of coffee from the vending machine down on the tiny table.

"Lucky me," Mel muttered.

"Lucky you."

Silence settled.

"How're the fingers?" he asked.

"I'll live," she said, lifting her hand, which had doubled in size thanks to the gauze and tape that covered the fifteen stitches that had been required to close up three of the fingers.

"That's good." He sipped the coffee, which apparently wasn't for her. "Any word on your mother?"

"Still in surgery. Bullet bounced off her pubic bone."

"Ouch."

"Ouch," she confirmed.

He took another sip of his coffee.

"What do you want?" she asked.

"Nothing really. I just thought you might be interested in what we learned about Nelson."

"Oh?" Mel said, raising an eyebrow.

"You were right, he did lose his leg in Afghanistan."

"Told ya."

"But he wasn't a part of Joseph's team. He wasn't even a part of the US military."

Mel frowned.

"He was a mercenary or, as they prefer to be called, a private military contractor. PMC for those that like acronyms."

"Okay."

"Afghanistan is rife with them. Has been ever since the invasion. Iraq too. You remember the Blackwater scandal a few years ago?"

She shook her head.

"It was in Iraq. Contractors opened fire on civilians. Kind of made the public aware of the fact that contractors were being used. It wasn't a secret or anything, but it wasn't something that anyone boasted about either."

"And what, Nelson was part of that?"

"No, no, not that. But he was employed by a company that had some marks against them, one that operated heavily within the region that Joseph's team was in."

Mel waited, but nothing else followed. "And?" she asked.

"And what?" he asked.

"That's it?"

"What else were you hoping for?"

"Why did Nelson lie to me about being friends with him, and why did Joseph try to kill him the moment they came face-to-face?"

"That I can't tell you," he said.

She sighed.

"We'll learn more once they both wake up."

"You think they'll actually talk to you?"

"We'll see."

She let out another sigh and then got up to get her own coffee from the machine in the corner. "You have any change?"

"Change?" he asked.

"For coffee," she said.

"Oh, sure." He pulled out some quarters and brought them over to her.

She took them, put them into the machine, and made her selection.

"You know, we were thinking, you might be able to get some more info from Nelson once he wakes up."

"We?" she asked.

"Me and Vince."

"Vince?"

"My partner."

"Fuck that."

"Why? I thought you wanted answers."

"The only answer I want is to know why he killed my father and then kept me in a straitjacket for two weeks."

"We want to know why he did that as—"

"Bullshit!" she snapped, cutting him off.

He blinked.

"All you wanted was an arrest, one that could be broadcast to everyone to show that you did your job. You don't care about the why of any of this. As far as you all are concerned, your job is done."

"Our job is far from done," he said, voice a bit raised. "Yes, we wanted an arrest. *Needed* an arrest after the shooting. But that was just the beginning. Now we have to establish why he did this. See if anyone else is to blame."

"Anyone else?"

"The public is going to want answers. An arrest isn't enough. Never really has been. Fortunately, Joseph is still alive. If he had been killed, it would never end, especially with his military connections and the religious implications.

Conspiracy theories would go viral within hours and make all our lives a living hell."

"My life already is a living hell."

He didn't reply to that.

"So, you want my help in getting answers."

"I just figured you might want to get to the bottom of things. For closure. And that Nelson would be a good place to start."

"I'd rather talk to Joseph," she said.

Higgins let out a humorless laugh and said, "That's not going to happen."

"Why not?"

"He's a suspect, one that is probably going to get a really good attorney who will work the case free of charge simply for the publicity. You going in to speak with him...that will be like a dream come true for the defense."

"But not me speaking with Nelson?"

"He's not being charged with anything."

"Yet," Mel said.

"I think it's pretty safe to say that our focus is going to be on Joseph. Whatever happened in Afghanistan is way beyond our jurisdiction."

"And I think it's pretty safe to say that I shouldn't trust a thing you say, and that I'm not going to do anything to try and help." With that, she picked up her coffee and was about to head over to the far corner of the waiting area but then stopped when the door opened.

Her mother's surgeon stepped in.

"Is she okay?" Mel asked, panic appearing.

"Yes, she's fine. Everything went really well."

"Can I see her?"

"Not yet. She's in recovery."

"How long?"

"Until she wakes up. At that point, they will move her into a room and you'll be able to see her."

"So what, I just keep waiting in here until then?"

The surgeon looked from Mel to Higgins and then back to Mel. "Here or in her room, or down in the cafeteria, which should be serving breakfast soon. It's really up to you."

Mel didn't know how to reply to this.

"Do you know what room she'll be in?" Higgins asked.

"Someone should be by to let you know," he said.

"That's it?" she asked, eyes going from the surgeon to Higgins. "You just come in here, tell me she is fine, but then don't give me any details?"

The surgeon was a bit taken aback by this.

"What did you want to know?" he asked.

"How long will the recovery be? Will she be able to walk? Use the bathroom? Shower? Will she need someone to stay with her to wipe her ass?"

"Whoa, whoa, this is all stuff they will talk to you about once she wakes up and is in her room."

"But what can you tell me? You're the surgeon. What can we expect?"

"I can't really say at this point. We need to watch her for a while, see how the recovery goes. Everyone's body is different. Generally speaking, it will be a difficult recovery. She will be in a wheelchair for a while and then will have to go through physical therapy. Bathing on her own won't be possible. Same with going to the bathroom."

"Jesus," Mel said, mind envisioning the ordeal.

A realization followed, one that made her grin.

No boarding school.

Not when her mother would need her at her side as a caregiver.

"Mel," Higgins said. "Mel?"

She blinked. "Yeah?"

"Did you have any other questions?"

Mel looked from him to the surgeon and shook her head.

Relief appeared on the surgeon's face.

"So, you hungry?" Higgins asked.

"What?"

"Hungry? Breakfast. I know I could use some food, and I'm sure you could too."

"No," she said, shaking her head. "I can't eat."

"Come on," he urged. "Get out of this waiting room for a bit."

She shook her head.

"Trust me, it'll be good for you. Plus, once you smell the food, you'll realize you're hungry."

"What part of no don't you understand?" she snapped.

"Fine," he said, holding up his hands. "Suit yourself."

JOSIAH BLINKED several times before the room came into focus. It was a medical bay, one that seemed a bit dark, the only lights being those down at the far end where a group of medical personnel were huddled.

An IV was present in his right arm, while a nasal cannula was strapped to his face. Something else was present beneath the sheets, something that he could not make out beyond the fact that it was invasive.

Pain hit.

Not a subtle pain, but an agonizing one that caused him to groan.

Hearing this, a young woman in colorful scrubs hurried over, soothing words leaving her lips.

They didn't help.

He screamed.

More soothing words, all while buttons were pressed on the machine that sat next to him.

The pain faded, as did his consciousness.

THE NEXT TIME he opened his eyes he was in a room with a TV, window, and door, one that was bright with sunlight.

Morning?

It felt that way, but he couldn't be sure given that he had no idea which direction the window was facing.

"Morning, Joseph," a voice said.

Josiah twisted a bit and realized that a man was sitting in a chair to his left, a man who would have been within his reach had it not been for the handcuffs that secured his left wrist to the bed frame. Not that he would have gone for him with the hand; his mind simply liked to calculate the potential for such actions.

"Sorry about that, but it seemed necessary given everything that has happened these last several weeks," the man said, nodding toward the restraints.

Josiah looked over at his right hand, which was not cuffed but had been immobilized by a splint and gauze so that it could hold various IVs that were attached to the IV pole.

He studied the various bags, but beyond the saline one, could not figure out what they were. Before the incident he would have known, given his training, but now it was like that part of his mind had been wiped.

"Joseph?" the man questioned.

"Who are you?" Josiah asked, head slowly turning back toward the man.

"My apologies. My name is Higgins. I'm an investigator with the Fox Hill Police Department. Do you mind if I ask you some questions?"

"Are you part of the Seven?" Josiah asked.

"No, but that was one of the things I wanted to ask you

about since you mentioned it last night. Do you mind if we talk about that?"

Josiah thought about this for a few seconds, his initial answer being a firm no, but then he remembered that an interrogation could be a two-way street, especially if the one doing the interrogation wasn't very skilled. Depending on the questions that were asked, he might learn more about the enemy than the enemy learned about him.

"I don't mind," he said.

"Good," the man said, faking a smile. "Great. I'm really glad to hear that."

Josiah faked his own smile and then grimaced as he shifted himself a bit.

"You okay?" Higgins asked.

"Yes," Josiah said and then asked, "Do you know how I make the bed go up? I want to sit up."

"Are you sure? You were stabbed in the belly. Folding yourself like that might be painful."

"I'm sure," he said.

"Well then, I believe it is that button on the device there," Higgins said while pointing.

Josiah followed his direction and said, "Ah, thanks," even though he had been fully aware of the device, its location, and how to use it. "Can you move it over here by my hand for me."

Higgins hesitated and then complied, his caution obvious as he reached across Josiah to take hold of the device on the right side and moved it over to his left hand.

"Thank you," Josiah said and fingered the button that lifted the top part of the bed.

Pain appeared with the movement, but it wasn't too extreme, likely due to the painkillers he was on. He wondered what they were and whether they would take him off them if he asked.

"Those burns on your hand, forearm, and face?" Higgins questioned. "Are they from the war?"

Josiah nodded.

"Roadside bomb?"

Josiah shook his head.

"Oh?"

"Oil lamp," Josiah said, mind struggling not to get sucked into the memory.

"Really?" Higgins said. "Wow. Was it an accident or intentional?"

Josiah thought about that for several seconds and then said, "Both."

"Both?"

Screams echoed as the memories arrived.

No! No! No!

"She thought I was one of them," he said, his heart beginning to race.

"One of whom?" Higgins asked, eyes going from him to the heart monitor and then back to him.

"Nelson's team. They had been raping her."

Gunshots echoed and then his skin was burning.

Josiah struggled against the bed, his left wrist pulling at the handcuffs while his right tried to pat out the flames.

Something tore free.

He screamed, not from the small sting as the IV ripped his skin, but from the flames that were eating away his flesh.

Voices echoed as medical personnel flooded into the room.

Someone jabbed him with something.

He didn't know what it was, but it somehow encased him in a softness that his mind could only visualize as a cloud.

MEL WANDERED THE HOSPITAL, her mind unable to cope with sitting in her mother's room watching her sleep, the morning TV nothing but news-themed stations or Oprah-style talk shows.

Hunger accompanied her, regret that she hadn't taken Detective Higgins up on his offer of breakfast making itself known.

She needed money.

And her phone.

Both were back in her room at home, one that she could not get to without getting an Uber, which she couldn't contact without her phone.

She was stuck.

It would have been amusing if it weren't so frustrating.

"They're talking about you on TV," a soft voice said as she got onto the elevator.

Mel looked at the young girl who had spoken, her eyes startled by her skeletal appearance. An oxygen tank was in a tiny side pack that the girl had slung over a shoulder, the clear tubes hooked around her ears and going up her nose.

"They say you shot the crazy guy up on fourteen," the girl added.

"Did they?" Mel asked.

"Uh-huh."

"Well, I didn't shoot him."

The girl stared at her.

"I stabbed him."

Shock appeared, her eyes going wide.

"He's a bad man though, so I wish I had shot him," Mel added.

"Did he hurt you?" she asked, pointing at her bandaged hand.

"Actually, I hurt myself while stabbing him."

The young girl contemplated that.

"Fifteen stitches," Mel said.

"Whoa!" She began to cough.

Mel winced at the wetness of the coughs, and then began to panic as the girl's face turned red, her right hand bracing herself against the elevator wall while the other tried to hit her own back.

The elevator doors opened.

Still coughing, the girl motioned to her to do something.

"What?" Mel asked, unsure what she was indicating.

"Holda."   Coughing.   "Holdadoor."   Coughing. "*Hold...door.*"

"Oh!" Mel spun and put her arm out as the doors began to close, stopping them.

"Thanks," the girl muttered, the coughing coming to an end.

"Are you okay?" Mel asked.

"Yeah, I'm fine." She took a wheezy breath and then grinned. "Hodor."

"What?"

"Hodor." Another wheeze. "Hold the door."

Mel shook her head.

"*Game of Thrones.*"

"I've never seen it."

"What? Jeez. You need to watch it."

"Okay."

"Seriously. It's, like, the greatest show ever. For my Make a Wish, I want to see if I can meet Arya."

"Arya?"

"She's a kid on the show. Totally badass." Another wheeze. "And now she is killing people like crazy. Revenge for her family. It's great." Her eyes got big. "Hey, you're kind of like Arya since you stabbed a bad guy."

Mel wasn't sure how to reply to that and simply smiled.

"Anyway, I got to get back. Breathing treatments."

"Good luck."

"You too."

With that, the girl slowly left the elevator and started down the hallway toward whatever room she was in, Mel watching until the doors closed, the number six button that she had hit upon her entry into the elevator still lit up.

She considered hitting number fourteen, her finger actually reaching for it before she dismissed the idea.

A few seconds later, the doors opened on six.

Mel hesitated.

Will he even be awake?

Only one way to find out.

She stepped off the elevator and started down the hallway.

JOSIAH OPENED HIS EYES.

The detective was gone, though the chair he had been waiting in remained.

He stared at it for a few seconds and then shifted his gaze toward the handcuffs that secured him to the bed frame.

Getting free was going to be tough.

Breaking the bed frame was not an option. Instead, he would have to break his thumb.

Or...

He leaned over to see if he could touch his hand with his mouth.

It was doable, though moving about was painful, the wound to his belly feeling like it could open up at any time.

Wait a few days...

No.

They could come for him anytime, the vulnerability of his situation one that they would not ignore.

He had to get free.

He had to endure.

The pain would be intense, both when he got free from the

handcuffs and when he got to his feet to escape, but it wouldn't kill him.

Nope.

The surgeons had patched him up and pumped him full of antibiotics, so unless something horrible happened, he would be fine. He would just have to make sure to keep things gentle once he got away from the hospital and the police. Once he got the little girl, found a place to recover, and could rest for a few days, he would be fine.

Someone came into the room.

Josiah expected to see the detective again. Instead, it was a young woman in scrubs and a lab coat.

"Joseph?" she said.

"Josiah," he corrected.

"Josiah?" she questioned.

"My name," he said. "It's Josiah."

"Oh, I see," she said. "Josiah." She nodded. "I'm Dr. Barclay. I worked on you last night when you came in."

Josiah didn't reply.

"I wanted to go over your injuries with you and let you know what to expect."

"Okay."

The next ten minutes were quite informative as Josiah learned that his small bowel had been punctured in three places when he had been stabbed, but not severed completely, which was good. They had also removed his appendix while they were in there, just in case the trauma caused it to rupture. As far as his chest went, the knife had gotten deflected by his ribs. A painful wound, but not a serious one. All in all, he had been lucky, according to the surgeon.

"God was watching over me," he said.

"I'd say so," she agreed. "Do you have any questions?"

"Yes, I do," he said. "My IVs. Which is which?"

Another few minutes came and went, Josiah noting what each IV bag contained.

"And why is that one dark?" he asked.

"Light can damage the antibiotics, so it's wrapped in a protective shield."

"I see," he said. "Actually, I think I remember that from Afghanistan."

"Oh?" she questioned.

"We learned how to do our own IVs," he said.

Shut up!

They don't need to know that.

Too late.

Making the slip-up worse, Detective Higgins walked in at that moment and asked, "What about Afghanistan?"

"JESUS CHRIST, YOU LOOK LIKE SHIT," Mel said.

"Yeah, well, you should see the other guy," Nelson said, his voice coarse.

"I did. He looked fine...until I stabbed him in the stomach."

Nelson perked up a bit. "You kill him?"

"No," she said. "I tried. Went to stab him in the chest, but the blade got caught and I ended up slicing my own fingers." She held up her bandaged hand. "Hurt like a motherfucker."

"Like O.J."

"What?"

"O.J. Simpson. They said he cut himself while stabbing his wife. Fingers slipped over the blade."

Mel didn't reply.

"Never mind. Before your time. Plus, the jury didn't buy it, so..." He waved a hand. "Tell me what happened."

"You first," she said.

"Me? You were there."

"Not in Afghanistan."

Nelson stared at her, her eyes able to see a bit of concern in his own.

"You lied to me," she added.

"What?"

"You weren't part of his team. You weren't even a soldier."

"Who told you that?"

"The police."

He considered this for a few seconds, his fingers gently scratching at the bandages on his face.

Mel waited.

"So what?" he muttered.

"So what? You lied to me!"

"Eh, a white lie at most," he said, finger getting under one of the bandages. "I was still there and we still knew each other. We just weren't on the same team."

"You said you were friends with him, that he saved your life."

"He did and we were."

"Explain," Mel said.

Nelson didn't reply right away.

"I'm waiting," she said and crossed her arms, a slight grimace escaping her lips as she put too much pressure on her bandaged hand.

"I was in a small convoy that came under attack. We had some detainees that were considered a priority. Joseph's team was in the area and came to our aid. He took out three guys that had me pinned down. After that, we got to talking and found out we were both from the St. Louis area and had both been part of the invasion of Iraq. I was SF at the time, and he was a soldier that eventually went SF after a couple tours. By then I was a contractor. He seemed interested in what I did, so we got together quite a bit and talked about it. I think it was the money. He lost everything in 2008. His sister had been investing his paychecks for him. Badly. Fortunately for him, he had the military, but she did not. He helped her stay afloat with his income, but it wasn't enough. Becoming a contractor would have solved everything for him. It's no secret that we are paid way more than active soldiers, and we pretty much do the same thing. Sadly, he was burned before he even finished with the military. The rest is history."

"Then why did he try to kill you last night?"

"I don't know. Maybe his mind is so fucked from the attack that he sees me as responsible. I was there. I tried to save him when that girl hit him with the lantern. But all his wires have been crossed to the point where he doesn't understand the reality of what happened."

"Hmm, could be," she said, but didn't really think this was the case. At least not in its entirety. Something more was at play between the two. She could sense it.

"So, any idea where he went after you stabbed him?" Nelson asked.

"Here," she said.

"Here?"

"Yeah, I didn't kill him, but he was in bad shape and couldn't get away this time. They were actually doing surgery on him at the same time as my mother."

"What happened to your mother?"

"He shot her. Right into the pubic bone. It was pretty bad."

"Jesus."

"Oh, and I pepper-sprayed a cop."

"You what?"

"I heard something and didn't realize it was the police officer dropping a deuce in the bathroom and kicked in the door while spraying him."

Nelson laughed at that, which then caused him to groan.

"You okay?" she asked.

"Yeah, just...ugh, never try to laugh with a broken face."

"I never plan on having a broken face, so..."

NELSON NEEDED TO KILL JOSEPH. It was the only task on his agenda. Had been ever since the news stories broke about the man having kidnapped Melinda and shot up the old folks' home. Kill him before he was arrested and could potentially spill the beans on what really happened that day with the girl in Afghanistan.

Why the company thought Joseph would talk about that day after all these years was beyond him, but they had offered Nelson a clean slate with the company and all his medical bills for the leg paid for if he succeeded, which was all that mattered. Nelson would never be out in the field again—they had made that perfectly clear—but being able to have a position within the company's headquarters after having been cut loose and left to fend for himself during his recovery all those years ago was fine with him.

Trouble was, he needed to kill Joseph in a way that didn't cause any blowback on the company itself. And now with the man laid up in a hospital bed under guard, this would prove problematic.

Not impossible though.

Nothing ever was.

First things first, he needed to know where Joseph was being kept and how many police officers were guarding him.

"WHAT ABOUT AFGHANISTAN?" Detective Higgins asked.

"Josiah here was telling me about IVs," Dr. Barclay said.

"Josiah?" Detective Higgins questioned.

"That's what Joseph prefers to be called."

"It's my name," Josiah said, a bit miffed at the way they were discussing him as if he were a child.

"I see." He turned to face Josiah. "Why Josiah?"

"It's my true name," Josiah said. "The one the Lord wanted me to have."

"Sort of like an Islamic war name?" Higgins asked.

"A what?" Josiah asked.

"A war name. Islamic soldiers take on names when they go to war. You've done the same, just in a Christian way."

"I suppose you could view it that way."

"So why did you choose the name Josiah?"

"I did not choose it. It was given to me."

"By Father Preston?" Higgins asked.

Josiah hesitated for several seconds and then nodded.

"Let's talk about that," Higgins said and took a seat.

"YOU SURE IT'S OKAY?" Mel asked, her concern genuine.

"Yeah," Nelson said while taking a test step, his body using the IV pole as a sort of crutch while testing out the old leg. "I'm supposed to be walking a bit every day anyway, and heading out like this is the only way I can get a soda."

"But what if you fall?" she asked.

"I won't."

"But what if you do?"

"It's a hospital. They pretty much have wheelchairs on standby in every corner of this place." He took another step. And then another. "Ugh, now I remember why I got a new leg."

"Pretty bad?"

"This one just never sat right," he said. "Doesn't matter how well strapped in it is, I feel like I'm sliding a bit with every step. It's disconcerting. And hard to describe. Just imagine taking a step and then feeling part of yourself sort of slip forward a few inches, almost like a car that is braking but still burns a bit of gas."

"Any idea when you'll get a new one?" she asked.

"No," he said. "It hasn't really been a focus yet."

"Wait," she said, stopping. "How'd you get this one?"

"It was in my trunk."

She stared at him.

"I always keep a spare leg in the trunk, don't you?" he added.

She shook her head. "How did you get it though? Your car was all the way over at Dr. Fletcher's house."

"Oh, the police brought it to me. That detective. What's his name? Higgins, I think. Nice guy, though I suspect the only reason he agreed to grab it for me was so he could search my car." He stopped walking and steadied himself. "He could have gotten a warrant easily, I'm sure, but me giving him permission made it simpler." He looked around. "Crap."

"What's wrong?" Mel asked.

"We're going the wrong way."

"Wrong way?"

"I want a soda." He turned. "But the machines are down that way."

"Oh."

They turned and started retracing their steps.

"You have enough money for two?" Mel asked after a few seconds.

"Yeah."

"Good, because I'm thirsty and hungry and have no money because I came here in my pajamas."

"Oh shit. You want to head down to the cafeteria and grab something?"

"Can you make it that far?"

"Maybe..." he started and then, "no, probably not. But I can give you some cash so you can get something."

"You sure?"

"Yeah. Can't let you starve to death."

"Thanks."

"There is just one condition."

"What?"

"Find out what room Joseph is in."

"Why?"

"I want to see him."

"They won't let you."

"They won't know."

Mel stared at him for a moment and then said, "I know he's up on fourteen, but beyond that I'll have to ask around."

"Okay."

Nothing else was said until they reached the machines, Nelson getting his soda while Mel now declined and said she would grab one while down in the cafeteria. Following that, they started back toward the room, Nelson having to pause several times.

"You need a chair?" Mel asked.

"No, no, I'm fine. Just dizzy."

"I think then it would be best if you had a chair."

"No, it passes."

Mel waited several seconds and then said, "You know, if you can barely walk down the hallway to get a soda, how are you going to make it to Joseph's room?"

Nelson gave her an exhausted grin and said, "Maybe by then I'll agree to let you push me in a wheelchair."

"Fuck that. I'm not pushing your ass anywhere."

This caught the attention of a middle-aged woman who was passing by, one who scoffed at her.

Mel turned, arms crossed, waiting.

Nothing.

The middle-aged woman glared for a moment and then walked away.

"Uh-oh, I think I'm wanted back in my room," Nelson said.

Mel turned and looked down the hallway.

"Ugh," she voiced.

"What?" Nelson asked.

"That's Detective Simmons," Mel said. "He's the one that laughed about you being beaten with your own leg."

"Hmm."

"He's a chauvinistic pig."

"Wonder what he wants."

"Probably is going to ask you if you and Joseph were fighting over who gets to fuck me."

"What?"

"That was his big theory on why Joseph attacked you. Jealousy."

"Well then, I guess I'll need to set him straight."

"Good luck. Let me know how it goes."

"You don't want to join in on the fun?"

"No. I think I'll head down and have—oh fuck."

Detective Simmons had spotted them and started heading their way.

JOSIAH COULD TELL that Detective Higgins didn't believe a word he was saying and that his nods were simply a way of humoring him so that he would continue talking. As infuriating as this was—he wanted to simply grab the man by the shoulders and shake him while screaming, "Can't you see!"—he continued answering the questions, his mind knowing that sooner or later the man would let something slip.

It happened while they were discussing New Eden.

Higgins wanted to know how he had discovered the abandoned facility and why he had decided to use it as a fallback position should anything happen.

"It was supposed to be for the Father," Josiah said. "I was trying to rebuild the chapel for him so that it would be ready once the End Times began to unfold."

"Did he instruct you to do this?" Higgins asked.

"No."

"Why New Eden?"

Josiah shrugged.

"What about the three kids you had captive there?"

"Kids?"

"Well, young adults. Two men tied to posts and a female handcuffed in a closet. One of the men was already dead. The other died on his way to the hospital."

"What about the girl?" Josiah asked.

"She'll be okay, once she gets rehydrated and then clean. Poor thing has been hooked on pain meds and heroin ever since a C-section got infected."

Josiah processed that, understanding of how addicting pain meds could be unfolding.

"Why were you holding them captive?"

"They simply showed up one day and said something about cooking, so I figured they were scoping out the place to set up some sort of drug lab."

"Was this before or after the eclipse?"

"After."

"Why did you torture them?"

"I needed to know if anyone else was going to show up so that I could prepare to defend the place if necessary."

Higgins raised an eyebrow.

"I didn't enjoy it," Josiah added.

"Not even just a little?" he asked.

"No."

"What about when you kidnapped Melinda? Did you enjoy having her locked up in that bedroom, chained to the bed?"

"I don't like what you're implying."

"What am I implying?"

"You know what you're implying."

Higgins waited.

Josiah stared.

"Why did you kidnap her?" Higgins asked.

"She showed up at her father's house while I was there," he said.

"Why take her with you? Why not just kill her?"

Josiah hesitated and then said, "I didn't know what to do with her and thought the Father might have some instructions for me once I let him know about her."

"Did he?"

"I never got a chance to speak with him. I tried, but they wouldn't let me near him."

"This was before the eclipse?"

"Yes."

"And then she got away from you?"

Josiah nodded.

"Let's go back to New Eden. Once you went there after the eclipse, what was the plan?"

"I had no plan. I was waiting for a sign."

"A sign?"

"From the Lord."

"And did you receive one?"

"Not yet," he lied.

"I DON'T WANT to talk to you," Mel said.

Detective Simmons shrugged. "I'm here to talk to Nelson, not you." He turned to Nelson. "We can either do this in your room or over there." He pointed to some chairs.

Nelson nodded toward the chairs.

Mel watched as the two headed that way, her own body refusing to turn and walk away.

Simmons looked at her and said, "You can join us if you want."

"Where's Detective Higgins?" she asked.

"He's currently conducting an interview with the suspect."

"By himself?"

"Yep."

"Isn't that, like, against the rules or something?"

"What rules?"

"I don't know. You're partners, so you always go in as a pair."

"Miranda Rights are the only rules we need to follow, and he waived them. So now Higgins will interview him first, and then I'll go in later."

"Ah, so you're doing a good cop, crap cop routine."

Simmons smiled.

Mel waited for a rebuff, but the smile seemed to be it, so she turned and headed toward the elevators.

JOSIAH WAS GROWING weary of the questions and decided to make it seem like he was drifting off from the various medications and painkillers that were flowing into his bloodstream.

Detective Higgins fell for the ploy and left.

Alone again, Josiah studied the handcuff link that secured his wrist.

Picking the lock would be ideal, but such a skill was not one that he had learned, so he dismissed it. Instead, he would resort to one of the oldest, most basic escape tactics that nature employed—chewing away the obstruction.

In his case, it would simply be some scar tissue.

So much had built up on his hand and wrist that once it

was chewed away, the cuff link would slide right off. Getting to that point would be a bit of an ordeal, given how painful and messy it would be, but he would be able to endure.

And once he was free...

He had to go get Lyn's daughter.

And bring her where?

No answers followed.

Just get the kid and then figure out how to protect her from the Seven.

Sins?

Could that really have been what the Father meant?

Was Josiah simply meant to find the girl and raise her in the light of the Lord, free from temptation?

Was that why he needed to purify himself first, so he could lead by example?

If so, it seemed so... anticlimactic.

Josiah was a warrior, not a babysitter.

A man of action.

The Fire of the Lord.

He didn't know the first thing about raising a kid, let alone raising one so that she was free from sin.

Was such a thing even possible?

It must be, a voice said.

Anything is possible with faith.

Josiah nodded to himself and then looked at his wrist.

Getting free needed to be his priority, first from the handcuffs and then the hospital itself. After that, he could focus on securing the girl and protecting her from the Seven. Sins? People? It didn't matter. He would simply protect her from everything and everyone once he had her. It would be a dull life, but one that would serve a higher purpose. She would probably hate him for it, but that would be okay.

Focus!

The word was like an explosion within his mind, one that might have been from the Lord himself.

He blinked as the echo faded and then shifted his body so that he could begin the process.

Hesitation hit just as he was about to sink his teeth into the mound of flesh.

Chewing away the scar tissue would produce quite a bit of blood, which would call attention to itself if anyone came into the room. And between the nurses, doctors, and detectives, people were coming in all the time.

He looked at the window.

Could he wait until nightfall?

Did he really have a choice?

What if someone came in to kill him before that?

Just because the Seven could simply mean sins rather than people, it didn't mean enemy soldiers weren't out there. At that very moment an assassin could be creeping down the hallway toward his room, ready to end his existence.

He needed to be ready for that.

He needed to be free.

ONCE AGAIN, Mel found herself staring at the number fourteen button on the elevator, a grumble from her stomach telling her to forget about Joseph and just focus on food, while the curious part of her mind urged her to press the button so she could try to see him, her hope being that his face was etched with pain.

She pressed the button.

The elevator brought her up to fourteen without stopping for any new passengers.

The doors opened.

With them came surprise.

It looked like a normal floor.

No gates were present, no doors with signs that warned about needing an escort because prisoners were kept beyond it. Nothing. It looked like a normal floor because it *was* a normal floor.

She stepped out of the elevator and started toward the nurses' station that was set in the middle of the floor, not so she could talk to them, but simply because she had to walk that way to get into the actual hallway.

Detective Higgins appeared from the right.

She halted.

He didn't see her, though only because he was asking a nurse a question, one that prompted her to look at a chart and then say something to him.

Mel slipped by him and started down the hallway.

No one tried to stop her.

No one seemed to care.

A normal floor.

A cop was sitting in a chair at the end, one who glanced at her as she approached and then went back to reading a magazine.

That was it. A single cop. Guarding a trained killer who was huge and had easily killed several people during the last two months.

Anger arrived.

How many times were they going to underestimate this guy?

How many more people did he have to kill before they took him seriously?

How many—

"Melinda!" a voice called. "What are you doing?"

She turned.

Detective Higgins was coming her way.

"One cop?" she demanded. "After everything he has done? One?"

"Whoa! Whoa! Whoa!" he said, holding a hand up. "It's okay."

"It's not okay!" she shouted.

"Come on," he motioned. "You'll see. He is heavily sedated and restrained. And in a lot of pain."

Mel stared at him for a moment, and then shifted her gaze to glance at all the people who had stopped to stare at the commotion, a few of them looking away when her eyes met theirs.

"Okay," she said, voice soft. "Show me."

JOSIAH THOUGHT about feigning sleep once he heard that they were going to be coming into the room, but then decided against it so he could see the girl, his free arm quickly wiping away at his face just in case there was any blood on his lips from the chewing he had started.

The two entered the room, the girl quickly looking at him, her eyes locking with his.

Several seconds came and went.

Nothing was said during it.

Detective Higgins waited for a bit and then motioned for them to leave.

"No," she said, shrugging away his touch.

Josiah grinned at this.

"Why did you kill my father?" she asked.

"Mel, you can't be asking these things," Higgins said, gripping her arm.

"It's okay," Josiah said. "I waived my rights earlier, and even if a lawyer wanted to, they'll never be able to mount a defense that will get me off. I don't think I'll even waste time with a trial."

Higgins hesitated for several seconds, but eventually let go of her arm.

"Why?" she asked again.

"He tried to put a stop to my talks with the Father."

She waited a few seconds and then said, "That's it?"

"Yes."

She put a hand to her head. "There has to be more to it."

"I couldn't let him interfere, not when the Father was speaking for the Lord."

"Speaking for the Lord? He was a crazy old pervert with dementia, one who used to rape teenage girls in an attempt to create children that would be pure and bring about a new Christian generation."

"No," Josiah said. "Those stories were falsehoods spread by the church."

"Falsehoods?"

"And your father fell for them. He was a good man, but between the lies of the church and the hell your whore mother put him through, he was very conflicted and eventually gave in to the enemy. I had no choice but to eliminate him and anyone else that stood in our way."

She stared at him for several seconds and then said, "Nelson should have let you burn to death in that house in Afghanistan."

"Let me?" Josiah said, a familiar rage building. "He tried to kill me."

"Kill you?" she asked.

"After I pulled him off the girl he was raping."

"Mel, come on," Higgins said, once again grabbing her arm.

She shrugged him away.

"He knows," Josiah said, nodding toward Higgins. "The government lied about the incident. They'll lie about anything that could spoil the false image of the war that they have projected to the public."

"Then why did she burn you and not him?" Mel demanded.

"She was scared and I looked like them, given my clothes," he said.

Mel didn't reply.

"Ask him," Josiah said.

Mel still didn't reply.

"And look into his eyes when you do," Josiah added.

"Come on, Mel," Higgins said.

Mel did not resist this time.

"Don't trust him," Josiah warned before they left. "No matter what he says, Nelson is not your friend and is not here to help you."

Mel halted their retreat and looked at him. "Then why is he here?"

"To kill me."

"Good," she spat and left the room.

Josiah stared at the empty doorway for a bit and listened, hoping he might hear another tidbit of useful information.

Nothing echoed into the room.

One cop, he noted to himself while focusing his attention back upon his hand. Once he was free of the cuffs, he would have to contend with the man.

Or slip by him.

An idea formed, one that was quickly pushed to the sidelines as his teeth sank into a chunk of scar tissue.

Pain hit once he was deep enough to get at active nerves, the coppery taste of blood hitting his tongue as he sawed back and forth against the tough strands of flesh.

"COULD he be telling the truth about Nelson?" Mel asked once they were in a tiny sitting room off the hallway.

"Anything is possible," Higgins said. "Afghanistan is the

Wild West right now. Soldiers, contractors, drug dealers, sex traffickers, terrorists...all are operating in a country that has almost no infrastructure beyond two or three cities, and no real law enforcement beyond the military."

Mel thought about this.

"Did you know most of the world's heroin comes from Afghanistan? It's their biggest export, one that is encouraged by the Taliban, which is gaining quite a bit of ground outside of the cities. For all we know, Nelson's company could have had their hands in the industry. And even if they didn't, I still wouldn't be surprised if he and other members of his company were abusing locals. Accountability is pretty low over there. Anything goes in the tribal regions."

"But why would the military cover up something that a contractor did?"

"They may have been contracted with the government itself."

"Why?"

"To do the jobs they don't want the military doing."

"I still don't get why Nelson would show up here," Mel said. "If it was to help him like he said, then I get it, but all this —it just doesn't make any sense to me."

"Joseph could be right," Higgins said. "He could have been sent here."

"To kill him?"

Higgins nodded.

"But why?"

"To keep him from talking about what happened. Defense contracts are a big deal to these private military companies, and if word started to spread that a contractor with this partic-ular company not only raped a young girl in Afghanistan, but also almost killed a service member who was trying to stop him, it could seriously jeopardize their future involvement with the government."

"But the government already knows," Mel said.

"Yeah, but that's different than the public knowing."

"Jesus."

"Yeah."

"It's just one thing after another," Mel said. "All because he got lost and wandered into Father Preston's room one night during his first week of work."

Higgins nodded. "Welcome to my world."

Mel looked at him for several seconds and then demanded, "What's that supposed to mean?"

"Nothing," he said with a wave of his hand.

Mel stood, her stomach letting out a roar as she did.

"Have you eaten yet?" Higgins asked.

"Not yet."

"Jesus, you need to eat."

"I don't have any money."

"Come on," he said.

Mel really didn't want to continue spending time with him, but knew she really didn't have a choice at this point. She needed food.

JOSIAH SLIPPED the cuff free from his hand, the pain from the torn flesh somewhat muted by the success of freeing himself.

Following this, he waited.

And waited.

And waited.

No one came into the room.

It was odd.

Up until then, it seemed like he had had a visitor every half hour or so, either someone from the medical team or someone from the police.

Now, nothing.

Why?

Did they know he was going to try to escape?

How could they?

Maybe it was just a normal lull.

Call button.

One press and someone could come to his aid.

After that...

The Lord would guide him.

MEL WAS HALFWAY through a plate of eggs with bacon, hash browns, and toast when Higgins gave a slight jump and pulled out his phone.

"Detective Higgins," he answered.

Mel paused with a forkful of yolked-up hash browns near her lips.

"Really? Okay. I'll be up in a few minutes."

He put the phone away.

"Something to do with Joseph?"

"Yep. He wants to talk to me."

"Why?" she asked.

"Don't know." He finished his coffee and stood.

"Be careful," she said, an uneasy feeling having arrived.

Detective Higgins blinked with surprise and then said, "Don't worry."

TEN MINUTES.

That was how long Josiah felt he had between the nurse leaving and Detective Higgins's arrival.

Ten minutes to free his right hand from the wrappings that secured it to the splint that was supposed to keep him from inadvertently dislodging the IVs, the task somewhat tricky given the pain that was still dominating his chewed-up left hand.

Once free, he slipped the hand beneath the sheets, his fingers flexing several times in anticipation of reaching up and grabbing the detective.

One chance.

It was all he would have.

A quick grab of the throat, followed by a squeeze to crush his vocal cords, and he would be free.

Well...on the path toward freedom.

Leaving the room and then the hospital would be tricky.

Voices.

Coming toward the room.

One sounded like Higgins; the other was unfamiliar.

Not good.

Normally, taking on two people would not be a problem, but given his condition and the need for surprise and stealth, having two in the room would be far from ideal.

A third voice joined in, this one asking if it was okay to use the bathroom and grab a soda while they were in the room talking to the suspect.

Higgins said it was.

The cop?

Was he actually leaving his post for a few minutes?

If so, then this was an opportunity he couldn't let slip by. It didn't matter if there were two in the room. Getting by the cop in the hallway had been an obstacle that would have been the most difficult to surmount. And now it had been removed.

SOMETHING WASN'T RIGHT.

Mel had sensed this from the moment Detective Higgins had gotten the call, and now that he was gone, it seemed to get stronger and stronger with each passing second.

Why would he want to talk to Higgins?

What more could he have to say after everything that had already been said?

It doesn't matter.

Let them deal with it.

She couldn't.

Something wasn't right, and if he managed to get away again...

How?

He's cuffed to the bed and has a giant knife wound in his gut.

A few seconds came and went, but the feeling still didn't fade.

She stood.

Don't! an inner voice warned.

She ignored it and headed to the elevators.

"JOSEPH, this is my partner, Detective Simmons," Detective Higgins said. "He is going to join us this time around."

"Josiah," Josiah said.

"Oh, right," Higgins said and turned to Simmons. "Josiah is his Christian war name. It means 'Fire of the Lord.'"

"I see," Simmons said. He eyed Josiah. "I know you served in both Iraq and Afghanistan, but what war are you fighting now?"

"The only war that matters," Josiah said. "Between Heaven and Hell."

"Oh."

"You can disbelieve if you want, but eternal damnation awaits everyone should I fail."

"Is this what Father Preston told you?" Simmons asked.

"Yes."

"And you believed him?"

Josiah didn't reply.

"Josiah?" Higgins questioned.

"Thirsty," Josiah said. "All this talking." He motioned toward the Styrofoam cup on the tiny table by the IV stand. "I need more ice chips."

Higgins and Simmons looked at each other and then Higgins said, "I'll get you some more ice chips, but then you have to promise to answer all our questions."

Josiah nodded.

Higgins walked around the bed and grabbed the cup, eyes peeking inside. "There's some water in the bottom."

"Can't," Josiah said. "NPO. No fluids or foods. Just ice chips to wet my lips."

Higgins sighed and said, "Where do I get the ice chips?"

"From the nurses' station."

"Okay."

With that, Higgins took the cup and left the room.

Josiah eyed Simmons, who eyed him back.

"Gutted by a sixteen-year-old girl," Simmons said. "She's gotten the better of you twice now."

"Yeah," Josiah said. Then, "Can you do me a favor? Can you hand me the bed remote so I can lift myself up a bit? Easier to talk that way." He nodded toward the right side. "It slipped over the side."

Simmons leaned over to grab it.

Josiah sprang into action, his right hand jabbing upward and hitting the detective's throat to paralyze the vocal cords and then grabbing him by the tie and twisting him around before he could process anything, his left arm hooking around his throat in a T-bar hold and squeezing.

It only took a few seconds, the detective's body going limp and falling onto the bed.

Josiah moved quickly after that, the pain from his gut

almost dropping him to his knees as he stood, a dry heave arriving and then being suppressed.

He got control of himself, his mind blocking out the pain as he carefully moved around the bed, a tug suddenly alerting him that the catheter had gotten snagged.

Fixing that, he flipped the detective onto the bed, cuffing the left hand to the rail and letting it hang from the bedsheets, which he pulled up to cover the rest of the body.

Deep breath.

And then another, the pain from his stomach wound returning now that he was standing still and waiting.

It was intense, though nowhere near the agony he had been in for months after the fire.

This he could endure.

This he had to endure.

If he didn't, all of mankind would face the agony of the flame.

The door squeaked.

Higgins was returning.

Four steps and he would round the corner that housed the tiny bathroom and face the bed.

Josiah waited.

Higgins appeared, a statement of "I have your—" starting to leave his lips and then being stifled as Josiah punched him square in the face, the cup of ice chips falling.

A second later, Josiah had crushed his windpipe with his forearm.

Too easy, Josiah said to himself while dragging the body into the bathroom to put into the shower stall.

Still have to get out of the hospital.

God's will.

He looked at the detective's clothes while thinking about his escape, but knew right away that they'd be too small. Same with Detective Simmons's clothes.

He did take the gun though.

And then he saw that there was a hospital bathrobe hanging from a hook on the door of the bathroom.

He tried it on.

It just barely fit.

Next he looked at the catheter and contemplated what to do with it, his mind thinking it was simply in place so that he didn't have to get up to use the bathroom rather than a medical necessity, given that his bladder had not been damaged by the knife.

Or was it?

Would the surgeon have kept that from him?

She had told him about everything else, so...

He decided to worry about that later and hooked the bag to the belt on the bathrobe, his hope being that having it visible would divert attention from his face. It would also keep people at a distance.

Keys!

He would need them to leave the hospital.

They were hooked onto the detective's belt, along with extra clips for the pistol and a fresh pair of handcuffs.

A cell phone was also present.

He grabbed them all and put them into the pockets of the bathrobe.

Go!

Before the police officer returns to his post.

Josiah did just this, his heart racing as he stepped out of the hospital room, his bloody left hand tucked up into the left pocket of the bathrobe while the right hovered near the right pocket where the gun was hidden.

No one stopped him.

No one even acknowledged him as he walked down the hallway.

It was almost too good to be true.

At the elevators, he paused, a realization that he had forgotten to grab the IV bags that contained the antibiotics arriving.

This could become a problem.

Go back?

No.

Too late.

God's will.

The elevator doors opened.

His eyes went wide.

Mel's did too.

He pulled the gun and stepped into the elevator before she could cry out for help.

"GROUND FLOOR," Joseph said.

Mel nodded, but also hit the button for Nelson's floor, an idea forming.

"You won't get away," she said as the elevator started down.

"I will, and you're coming with," he replied.

"The fuck I am."

"God keeps putting you in my path. He means for you to help me. I didn't see it before. You and I are to raise the child together."

"What child?" she asked, eyes on the numbers.

Two more floors.

"Lyn's daughter. She is the one. I'm to protect her from the Seven and raise her. She will usher in the Lord's kingdom."

The elevator slowed and then stopped.

Joseph looked confused.

The door opened.

"Nelson!" Mel screamed at the top of her lungs and then lunged for the gun.

It went off, a bullet catching her in the arm.

The pain was unlike anything she had ever experienced before.

Don't let go, her mind cried.

She didn't, her body pulling back while hanging on to his gun hand, her leg kicking backward to try to keep the doors from closing, all while voices of panic echoed beyond.

It worked, but her strength was failing.

She couldn't hold on much longer.

Thankfully, he was in considerable pain as well and wasn't able to put up much of a fight.

Still, he was going to win.

She had to do something.

She couldn't let him get away again.

And then her eyes spotted the catheter bag hooked onto his belt.

She grabbed it and threw herself from the elevator.

Joseph cried out with the sudden pull.

"Let go!" he screamed.

She didn't.

The doors started to close, the tiny, thin cord not enough to keep them open.

Joseph's eyes went wide.

"No!" he cried, the doors shutting.

The bag was pulled from her hands as the elevator started to descend toward the ground floor, and then smashed into the doors, urine splattering everywhere as it was torn open.

Mel started to lose focus, the room spinning as people came to her aid, a distant scream reaching her ears as the elevator continued toward the ground floor.

PART FIVE
THE ACCIDENT

TWENTY-THREE

"MOMMY, ICE CREAM!" Nellie said, pointing to the shop across the busy street.

"I see it, sweetie, we're almost there."

"Ice cream!" Nellie cried, tugging at her hand.

"Sweetie, not until the light is green."

A buzz echoed in her pocket.

Lyn pulled her phone out with one hand while her other continued to grip Nellie's tiny hand.

She looked at the screen.

Bill.

"Hey," she answered after thumbing the Accept button.

"We're all dying to know," Bill said. "How'd it go?"

"Well..." she teased. "I have some bad news."

"Oh no."

"It seems Nellie and I won't be able to fly home tonight because they want to get her going into the commercials right away."

"Wait! What? So she got the part?"

"Yep!"

"Oh my God!" Then, away from the phone, he shouted, "Nellie got the part!"

Cheers echoed in the background.

Lyn grinned.

Bill came back on the line. "I'm sure you just heard all that."

"I think everyone on this street corner heard that," Lyn said, laughing.

"I'm still in shock about the whole thing."

"Me too," Lyn said and then felt a tug on her hand as Nellie tried to pull her into the crosswalk. "Honey, not until it's green," she scolded. Then, into the phone: "Who would have thought? My little girl is going to be a star."

All because of that stupid interview I almost didn't do...

A chill followed, along with memories of being kept hand-cuffed to a pipe in the supply closest of the abandoned mental institution. With the memories came a familiar need.

"Green! Green! Green!" Nellie cried.

"Is that Nellie I hear?" Bill asked.

"Yep," Lyn said, letting Nellie guide her into the cross-walk. "Little Miss Independent is leading the way as always, right to an ice cream place I promised to take her to after the meetings."

He laughed. "That sounds like Nellie."

"Honestly, I think she's more excited about the ice cream than scoring the part in the TV show—"

"Hey!"

"Stop!"

Brakes screeched.

Startled, Lyn turned just in time to see the grille of a giant bus bearing down on them.

The following are from the New York Chronicle:

Mother and Daughter Killed by Bus

A mother and her three-year-old daughter were killed today when the pair stepped out into traffic at a crosswalk. Witnesses say that the mother was talking on her cell phone when she allowed her daughter to lead her out into oncoming traffic.

Bus Driver Dies Following Accident

Walter Rainy, the bus driver who suffered a heart attack after hitting a mother and her three-year-old daughter in a crosswalk yesterday, has died. Investigators are still looking into the incident, but unnamed persons with the department have said this looks to be an unfortunate case of a distracted pedestrian stepping out into traffic against a red light.

Driver of the Number 7 Bus Cleared

Walter Rainy, who died following a heart attack after hitting two pedestrians in a crosswalk last Wednesday, has been cleared of any wrongdoing in the accident that claimed the lives of a mother and her three-year-old daughter.